WE ARE NOT ALONE...

The statistical odds *against* Man being the only form of
intelligent life in the Universe are enormous. Somewhere
in the immense vastness of outer space there must be
worlds – or other dimensions – where life has evolved far
beyond human levels. Such superior beings in all
likelihood have long since mastered techniques for
interstellar and intergalactic travel that are at present
literally light years beyond the grasp of earthly science.
The overwhelming evidence of the past thirty years
(millions of UFO sightings of various kinds by reliable
witnesses all over the world) indicates that such higher
intelligences have been watching human affairs intently.
And Government agencies of all nations are obviously
not telling the people the full story behind the whole
UFO mystery. The indications are that a major contact
between humans and alien beings is imminent – *if it has
not already taken place.*
From this mind-stunning foundation Steven Spielberg,
one of the handful of true geniuses operating in the
contemporary film world, has created a story that will not
only rank as the greatest imaginative motion picture since
2001 : A SPACE ODYSSEY but will also expand the cosmic
awareness of all who encounter it ...

Close Encounters of the Third Kind

STEVEN SPIELBERG

SPHERE BOOKS LIMITED
30/32 Gray's Inn Road, London WC1X 8JL

First published in Great Britain by Sphere Books Ltd 1978

'*When you wish upon a star*' from the film *Pinocchio*,
Music by Lee Harline, Words by Ned Washington.
Copyright 1940 Irving Berlin Inc (Now Bourne Inc),
reproduced by kind permission of Chappell & Co. Ltd.

Copyright renewed. Used by permission.

Copyright © 1977 by Dell Publishing Co., Inc.

All rights reserved. Published by arrangement with
Delacorte Press/Dell Publishing Co., Inc., New York

Printed in Great Britain by
Hazell Watson & Viney Ltd
Aylesbury, Bucks

ONE

Seven mis-shapen figures emerged from a blinding swirl of desert sand and sage. Their images hazing in and out of tons of gushing earth. Three somewhat stupefied *Federales* were waiting just outside the one-horse town of Sonoyita in Northern Mexico. Honking and tugging hysterically at their hitching place, the *burros* sensed another intrusion and kicked at everything in sight. The figures were almost upon them now and from shared views the first building in this haunted desert junction loomed ominously. Straight up, the sun said noon but its colour was blood, matching an antique neon Coca-Cola sign within the adobe frame of some Cantina oasis. The first figure out of the wind was just over six feet and greeted the three Mexican police with a curt nod and a barrage of Spanish. 'Are we the first to arrive?' the khaki-clad man shouted in high-school Spanish, his Rommel goggles and leather bandana hiding his nationality. 'Are we first here?' he demanded.

The stunned policeman answered him by nodding southward, where another group of explorers was materializing from thin air. And at the fringes of Sonoyita in a desert storm in 1973 the two teams came together, fourteen total, handshakes brief and voices discreet.

'Is the French interpreter with you?' The hidden face had an American voice, slightly bucolic, maybe Ohio-Tennessee. 'Yes, sir. I speak French but I'm not an interpreter by profession.' The voice belonged to the shortest member of the second-arriving group, and in it was the slightest suggestion of fear. Beefing up to compete with the wind howl, David Laughlin began to sound more important. 'My occupation is cartography, topographics. I'm a map maker. A map maker.'

'Can you speak French, sir? Can you translate English into French, French into English?'

'If you go slow and understand this is not what they pay me for.' Interrupting, another figure came forward and extended a hand to the cartographer and spoke broken English with an accent that was native French.

'You are monsieur . . . uh . . . Loog-oh-line?'

'Uh . . . Laughlin,' Laughlin gently corrected, and shook the hand. There was something about the Frenchman's voice that invited soft, careful responses.

'Ah, *oui*,' the Frenchman chuckled almost apologetically.

'*Oui, oui, pardon*.' And then, in French this time. 'And, Mr. Laughlin, how long have you been a project member with us?'

Laughlin was proud to answer that question and he chose his words carefully.

'From the time of my country's merger with the French in 'sixty-nine. I attended the Montsoreau talks the week the French broke through. My congratulations, Mr. Lacombe.' Lacombe smiled, but the team was itching to move on in anticipation of what they had come all this way to see. Sensing this, Mr. Lacombe led the way and began to converse with Laughlin as quickly as he went. He waved to another team member and in seconds Robert Watts, Lacombe's personal bodyguard, was in sandy step.

'Robert, *écoute* Monsieur Laugh-o-line.'

'Yes, sir.'

'Say to Robert in English, Mr. Laugh-o-line, this what I say to you now *en français. Alors.*' Lacombe rattled off a statement in French and Laughlin said it in English to Robert only a beat or so behind the spoken word.

'You are going to translate not only what I will say,' Laughlin enunciated, 'but also my feelings and my emotions. I must be understood perfectly.'

Up ahead the Mexican *Federales* were shouting and pointing at things in an area being pummeled now by forty-five-mile-an-hour winds. So much dirt blew across everyone's eyes that the first object intermittently resembled a dragonfly with a fifty-foot wingspan. The men approached cautiously and the phantom shape began to tell them what had only been hearsay twenty-four hours earlier.

Something was sitting in the road, on what looked like wheels with wings, tail and propeller. There were markings on the sides and numbers on the wing. Behind it when the red wind gave pause were six others just like it. They were Navy Grumman T-3 Avenger Torpedo bombers, circa World War II.

. The expedition came to a halt. Lacombe took several steps and lifted his smudged bubble goggles. There was a curious peace about him now. He seemed neither anxious nor passive as he gathered in the view. The Frenchman's face was incongruously youthful despite his grey, weedy hair.

Deep-cut lines started at his nostrils and ended at each side of his mouth. And as he made up his mind about what was to be done, the lines seemed to deepen. Lacombe took a breath, wiped dust from his tongue with the back of his hand, put on a sterile polyethylene glove and gave Laughlin his first order to relay. Laughlin nodded quickly after the spurt of words and shouted to everyone standing there.

'I want the numbers off the engine blocks.' Laughlin wondered if he hadn't made a mistake by not editorially attributing the command with the understood 'he'. No one seemed to care. In seconds, fourteen project personnel were crawling across the wings and tail opening hatches and unscrewing caps. Everyone wore Playtex living gloves. One technician rolled back the canopy. It slid open without a bump. The grooves and ball bearings good as new. With his polyethylene glove, one of the technicians used surgical tweezers to extract a calendar stuck under the instrument panel. The calendar was a promotional item: 'Trade Winds Bar, Pensacola, Florida.' But the date was the best part.

'Mr. Lacombe,' the gloved technician shouted breathlessly, on the brink of discovery. 'It's dated May!'

'*Quoi*?' Lacombe went right to Laughlin for the translation, but the technician was quicker. 'May through December 1948.'

Lacombe understood this only too well. He beamed and raised his voice to Laughlin. Laughlin blanched and hollered to everyone in English.

'See if there is petrol ... gasoline, in the tanks. See if the gasoline will support combustion.'

8

Standing next to Laughlin was the bodyguard, his arms sagging in wonderment.

'Jesus. These babies are in perfect shape.' A voice ripped the day apart in triumph. The voice sounded Southern.

'AE 3034567. Goddamn! AE 29930404. Christ! AE 335444536. Holy shit!' Laughlin left out the expletives and someone else checked the numbers against a sheet of paper.

'Numbers on the engine blocks match. So do the wing numerals.' The bandana that kept the sand from Lacombe's nostrils and throat rose high around his face, his eyes were on fire as someone tested one of the Grumman's landing lights. They cut a twin pattern in the thick air.

'*C'est possible*?' Lacombe was slapping his sides, and Laughlin, befuddled now beyond reason, nudged Robert, the bodyguard.

'Would you bring me up to date?'

Robert bent forward confidentially. 'It's Flight 19.'

'Go on.'

'Flight 19. Don't you know? This was the squadron of aircraft departed Pensacola on training manoeuvres in May '48. That was the last anyone ever saw of them. Until today. You figure it out.'

'But where are the pilots? Where's the crew?' Robert didn't have the answer, he just shrugged when unintelligible hollering commenced a few feet beyond this activity. Lacombe rushed over, Laughlin on his heels. The three *Federales* had a collar. A tiny form huddled in the threshold of the Cantina. The Mexican police wouldn't shut up, and all of their noise sounded like panic. Lacombe looked in

Laughlin's direction for a little help and David had to smile.

'*Je ne parle pas espagnol. Français et anglais seulement.*'

Mr. Tennessee-Ohio spoke up. 'They say this man was here. They say he was here two days. They say he saw it happen.'

This was more than Lacombe or anyone had hoped for. The Frenchman dropped to one knee and with the gentlest touch cupped the humbled chin in his sterile glove. The Mexican raised his head the rest of the way. He was crying but that wasn't what riveted Lacombe. Half of the man's face was cherry red and blistering from forehead to collarbone. It was the worst sunburn Laughlin had ever seen on a leathery face so accustomed to Mexico's furnace summers. The man's hands were buzzing and a certain stench drifted up that brought Lacombe's gaze to the Mexican's starched pants. He had urinated in them some time ago and as he lifted his face to speak, he was involuntarily wetting them again. The sad, desolate man worked his lips together, forcing air through his vocal cords, trying so hard to say it. And when the word broke in Spanish, the man broke down in real tears.

'*Qu'est-ce qu'il dit?*' Lacombe breathed. Laughlin turned to the American who knew the language. But the man shrugged and questioned the humbled wreck at his feet. Again the same word croaked forward and the smell of urine was unbearable. Lacombe was a patient man but the American was keeping the word to himself for too long a time. Laughlin intervened. 'What did he say? What was that word he said?' The American raised his eye-

brows and let out a sigh along with the translation.
'Music.'
    'What?'
    'That's all he said. Music. You figure it out.'

TWO

Four-year-old Barry Guiler was having a restless night. A gentle Indiana breeze floating through the half-open bedroom window ruffled his bangs. There was a soft but persistent whirring noise coming from somewhere in Barry's room, and it troubled his sleep. Suddenly a soft red glow played over his face and Barry's eyes opened.

On the nightstand next to his bed, one of Barry's battered toys had somehow come on. It was a Frankenstein monster: when it raised it's hands, as if to strike out, its pants fell down abruptly and its face blushed bright red.

Barry sat up in bed, staring at Frankenstein, and then looked around the room. He had a lot of battery-operated toys scattered about – a Sherman tank, a rocket ship, a police car with red dome light and siren, a model 747, a drunk hanging onto a lamp post and chugging from a bottle – and all of them were moving, flashing, whirring. All by themselves.

Barry was delighted. His phonograph came to life all of a sudden, scratching out a tinny version of the 'Sesame Street' theme song.

Barry laughed and clapped his hands together. Then he jumped out of bed and ran over to the open window. Outside, in the distance, he heard a dog barking, but his backyard was dark and utterly still.

Barry's bedroom was at the end of a hallway.

Very curious now, he trotted down the hall to the living room. The room was dark except for a small blue night light. Barry sensed, though, that something was different, something was out of place. All the living-room windows were wide open and the night air was breathing through the lacy curtains, stirring them in a very odd way. The next thing Barry noticed was that somehow the front door had got itself wide open, too, and the front porch light was shining brightly against the black night.

Despite all these strange things, the little boy was not frightened. He was ready for fun. There was a funny smell coming in the open windows and door. A little like the way the air smelled after there had been a lot of thunder and lightning. But Barry didn't think a summer storm had just come through. He hadn't heard anything; he didn't hear any water dripping. Besides, this was different.

He decided to go see what was happening in the kitchen. Wow! All the windows in there were wide open, too, and the breeze was really blowing. The back door was ajar and rattling against the safety chain. But that was nothing! Bingo's dog door had got knocked off its hinges and was lying on the floor, and Bingo wasn't in his bed next to the refrigerator.

The refrigerator was open, too, and there was a lot of food – a milk carton, some Cokes, butter, a cottage cheese container, bologna, leftover dinner – in messy piles on the floor in front of the ice box, leaving a sloppy trail all the way to the open dog door. Barry picked up a half-melted Heath Bar. Then something else in the kitchen caught Barry's attention. Several somethings. Barry spun. The

Heath Bar dropped from his open hand, splattering across the linoleum. The little boy backed away so quickly he slammed shut the big Amana with his tiny body. He carefully waited, his soft eyes unmoving. And then Barry Guiler smiled – a shy playful look that seemed to invite . . . a response. Barry looked some more – and giggled and looked away – peek-a-boo – more laughter – peek-a-boo. New Game. Barry looked hard; then, rocking back and forth on his heels like a chimpanzee, he spun full around, cocking his head to one side before rotating it slowly – 'Like this? Like this?' He was brave. 'Boo!' He shouted. And made his scariest face. 'Grrrrr-boo!' A scarin' face – his scariest.

Jillian Guiler had been asleep in her bedroom. Jillian had had the 'flu all week, and her head, her bed, and the room were all in a state of general disarray. The house that Jillian and Barry lived in was small and stood by itself atop a low, rolling hill in this rural area of Indiana. It was really an easy house to take care of, but Jillian had felt pretty rotten all week and had let the housework slide.

In her bedroom, everything was everywhere but where it should have been. The same wind that had been playing through the rest of the house suddenly swept into Jillian's bedroom, picking up and dropping Kleenexes and a couple of half-finished charcoal sketches of Barry. The bedside table was a clutter of pills, nasal sprays, half a sandwich, and a can of Coke.

Jillian started coming half awake in that peculiar frame of mind that 'flu produces: tired but not sleepy, thinking but not very clearly, able to do something but not about to. She was under the covers but was still wearing a bathrobe. The TV set was on, and the laughter Jillian at first heard she thought was coming from the stupid sitcom that she saw flickering on the screen. But during a commercial Jillian heard the laughter again and finally recognised its source.

Barry began to imitate the thing outside, mimicking what he saw. First he covered and uncovered his eyes, as if playing peek-a-boo. Then he spun around several times like a top. He cocked his head left and right and left and right again.

He began to laugh out loud with the joy of it, moving into the night as he did so. A pale, burnt-orange light illuminated his face as he walked into the night, laughing.

It was the laughter, growing fainter, that wakened Jillian at last.

Well, that and the parade of toys. The laughter brought her half awake, wondering what had disturbed her slumber. Then, as she sat forward, eyes slowly opening, the police car came through the door of her bedroom first, its dome light flashing.

Behind it rumbled the tank, fire flashing in its gun muzzle. Next the giant jumbo jet trundled forward to the accompanying whine of the police siren. And, finally, his pants dropping down, rising and falling again, Frankenstein's monster lurched in, arms outstretched.

Jillian jumped wide awake, flipped off her covers and got out of bed. The police car narrowly missed her toes as it headed for a wall and shoved its grill into the plaster. Behind it the other toys began piling up in a confused, multi-vehicle collision.

'Barry?' Jillian called.

16

Then she remembered his laughter. It had all but faded away, only the memory of it still hanging in the night air.

The bedside clock read 10:40. What in the world was Barry up to now? He'd only been in bed two hours.

Jillian staggered out of bed and went down the hall to her son's room. Barry's bed was empty. The windows were open. She ran out of the room, back down the hall to the living room. There she stared about her wildly at the open windows, the open front door, the shining porch light.

Unmistakably now, the sound of Barry's laughter was outside the house, out in the night somewhere. Jillian gave a little cry and then she sneezed.

The laughter again. Fainter this time.

Oh, God! Jillian thought wildly. She rushed out the front door into the yard. Trying unsuccessfully to adjust her eyes to the darkness beyond the porch light, Jillian found herself whimpering and then, catching hold of herself as best she could, she cried, 'Barry! Barry!' and ran into the darkness in the general direction of her son's disappearing laughter.

THREE

The world inside all air traffic control centres is unreal. There are dozens of them scattered across the United States: the one half-buried in the earth near Indianapolis is as typical as any.

The artificial world created within these great concrete bunkers is only dimly perceived. The place is dark. The only light comes from small, shaded bulbs of low wattage that barely show where the doors are.

Most of the light comes from radar screens that sweep the sky over Indiana's airspace. Here there is no day, no night, only an artificial gloom and the bright radar glowing its electronic picture of what is happening in the real world overhead.

The nation's air traffic passes in review, noted on radar, interrogated by radio, announcing itself, making proper identification, receiving approvals and advice, and either landing in Indiana airspace or, more often, passing above at speeds nearing 600 miles per hour to its destination elsewhere.

False as this dim world is, it presents what every air traffic controller hopes is an accurate picture of real events. He hopes that every jumbo jet, every low-flying Piper Cub, is duly noted and neatly notched into an arrangement that assures everyone safe passage through Indiana airspace.

That is the controller's hope. That is now what always happens.

Harry Crain was working midwatch that week.

On midwatch there were only five or six men at the radar scopes. Harry usually moved behind them, pacing back and forth or resting occasionally on a tall stool, his headset connected by a long coiled wire to the radio bands in use, a small curving plastic tube that picked up his voice and conveyed it by microphone to the real world high above his head.

This night, four controllers made up the front-line team. They sat side by side, in pairs, all in open-necked white shirts, the sleeves rolled up one fold, each pair watching their scope. Above their heads, loudspeakers squawked and rasped the usual radio air traffic drone, sparse now because in the airspace over Indianapolis it was now as black a night as it was in the air traffic control centre below.

'Air Traffic Control,' a pilot's voice came in. 'You have any traffic for Aireast 31?'

Harry Crain looked intently at one of the scopes. There were only three full data blocks and one partial data block. The two going in the same direction were fifteen miles apart; the third going in the other direction was a great distance away from Aireast. The rest of the scope was clean.

Harry cut his mike into the circuit. 'Aireast 31, negative. Only traffic I have is a TWA L-1011 your six-o'clock position fifteen miles and an Allegheny DC-9 your twelve o'clock fifty miles. Stand by one. Let me take a look at the broadband.'

Harry reached up and pushed a button. The radar scope changed from narrow band computer radar to broadband normal radar. Harry took a quick look, pushed the button again, then another button. He looked at the primary picture in computerised form. There *was* a non-beacon target in Aireast's vicinity. Harry peered at the scope more intently just as the pilot broadcast again. 'Aireast 31 has traffic two o'clock three to five miles, slightly above and descending.'

One of Harry's controllers leaned over, looked and grunted surprised confirmation.

'Aireast 31, roger,' Harry said. 'I have a primary target about that position now. We have no known high altitude traffic. Let me check with low.'

Harry turned to his interphone man and said, 'Call low and see if they know who this—'

'Centre, Aireast 31,' the pilot came back on, cutting through Harry. 'Traffic's not in low. He's one o'clock now, still above me and descending.'

'Can you tell aircraft type?'

The pilot's voice was matter-of-fact, considering the information he was about to report. 'Negative. No distant outline. The target is brilliant. Has the brightest anti-collision lights I've ever seen – alternating white to red and the colours are striking.'

The other sector controllers were now looking and listening. The coordinator reached up, pushed a button, called someone and mumbled indistinctly.

Harry sat back on his high stool for a moment and eyed the radar scopes. 'TWA 517,' he called to the other aircraft. 'Can you confirm?'

A different voice came over the loudspeaker. 'Centre, this is TWA 517. Traffic now looks like extra bright landing lights. I thought Aireast had his landing lights on.'

The coordinator said, 'What do we have here, Harry?'

'Say again, TWA 517,' Aireast asked.

The TWA pilot enunciated slowly and clearly. 'Do you have your landing lights on?'

'Negative.'

Harry broke in. 'TWA 517, Indianapolis Center. Aireast is your twelve o'clock position, fifteen miles same direction and altitude. Ident, please.' He turned to his coordinator, saying, 'Aireast claims he has unusual traffic almost at his altitude. I don't know who it is.'

The TWA identification appeared on the screen and Harry asked the pilot if he had the Aireast jet in sight.

'Affirmative.'

'TWA 517, do you have Aireast's traffic in sight?'

'Yes,' the pilot said cautiously. 'We have it now and have been watching it.'

'What does traffic appear to be doing?'

'Just what Aireast 31 said.'

Aireast 31 cut in. 'He's in a descent about fifteen hundred feet below me. Wait a second . . . Stand by one . . . Okay, Centre. Aireast 31 traffic has turned heading right for us at altitude. We're turning right and leaving flight level three fifty.'

Harry Crain jumped off his stool and everyone in the dim room tensed.

The coordinator turned and said, 'Get on the phone to Wright-Patterson and see what the hell they could be testing up there.'

'Aireast 31, roger,' Harry said at the same time. 'Descend and maintain flight level three-one-zero . . . Allegheny DC-9, turn thirty degrees right immediately . . . traffic twelve o'clock, two zero miles, Aireast jet descending to FL-310.'

The Aireast pilot, still remarkably low key, said,

'Luminous traffic now in angular descent and exhibiting some non-ballistic motions.'

Harry and his coordinator just looked at each other and said nothing.

'Okay, Centre,' Aireast said, conversationally. 'Traffic is coming on strong. Ultra bright and really moving.'

'This is TWA 517,' the other pilot said. 'We're going to go a little right to keep away from traffic also.'

'TWA 517, roger,' Harry Crain said. 'Deviations to right of course approved.'

'Centre, Aireast 31 is out of three-one-zero and traffic has passed off our ten o'clock, five hundred yards and really moving.'

The team supervisor, who had moved in the dim room to a point just behind Harry, spoke for the first time. 'Ask them if they want to report officially.'

'Aireast 31, roger,' Harry said. 'Report flight level three-one-zero. TWA 517, do you want to report a UFO?'

There was only static for several moments. Then: 'Negative . . . We don't want to report.'

'Aireast 31, do you wish to report a UFO?'

More static.

'Negative. We don't want to report.'

'Aireast 31,' Harry Crain persisted. 'Do you want to file a report of any kind?'

'I wouldn't know what kind of report to file, Centre.'

Harry smiled and started to relax. 'Me neither,' he said. 'I'll try to track traffic to destination.'

'And show us at level three-one-zero now,' the

pilot said, and then added, almost as an after-thought, 'The gals up here tell me that passengers were snapping pictures of traffic during that close pass.'

Harry Crain turned to his team supervisor and said softly, 'Those I'd like to see.' Then, speaking again into the microphone, he said, 'Allegheny Triple-four turn right to intercept J-8. Resume normal navigation. TWA is level at three-one.'

The team supervisor left Harry, disappearing again into the dimness. The tension sifted out of the centre.

Harry's coordinator asked, 'What's in the book about this kind of thing?'

'Hell if I know,' Harry Crain said. 'The Air Force started writing it thirty years ago. Let them finish it.'

FOUR

Aireast 31 passed over Roy Neary's home about nine o'clock that night, its jet engines sounding only faintly inside the house, and none of the occupants seemed to notice.

Roy had confiscated the family room of the suburban house and made it into a workroom that looked like a hobby room run by the Salvation Army. There were mechanised and electrical inventions that hung and lay abandoned along the walls and in the corners, and there were enough adult toys lying around to rob the children of their childhood.

The most prominent object in the room was an HO gauge railroad laid out on the family ping pong table. The tracks ran through elaborate Tyrolean terrain, complete with mountains and lakes.

That night Roy Neary and his eight-year-old son, Brad, were alone in the room, sitting side by side. Roy was trying to help Brad with his maths. Brad, a pile of arithmetic books on the floor at his feet, was considerably less interested in addition than in electric trains.

Neary had carefully explained to Ronnie, his wife, who enjoyed a game of ping pong now and then, that a model railroad was a necessity when there were growing boys in the family. 'A necessity for the father,' she had pointed out. 'Like ping pong is for the mother.'

Roy had finessed the potential confrontation by

promising to dismantle the railroads on weekends, but somehow, over the months, instead of being dismantled, it had grown in complexity, until it now took most of Neary's leisure time simply to keep it running.

'How about a drawbridge over that underpass?' Brad asked.

Neary frowned at his son. 'I thought you were supposed to be doing your homework.'

'I hate arithmetic.' The eight-year-old threw down his pencil and stared challengingly at his father.

'You're not trying.'

'Train engineers don't need arithmetic.'

Neary picked up the pencil and put it back in the boy's hand. 'Suppose,' he said, 'the station master assigns you eighteen cars. Then he says, "Make up two trains with the same number of cars in each." What do you do?'

Brad threw the pencil down again and reached into his rear pocket. Out came a Texas Instruments pocket calculator. 'It won't matter,' the boy said. ' 'Cause I'll have one of these.'

Roy sighed and looked heavenward. The long moment of silence between them was fractured by Toby Neary, six years old and a tornado, who carved a path of destruction into the room and yanked to a halt in front of his father. Toby was very angry. His blue eyes blazed, and he stuck a not-very-clean finger in Roy's face.

'You stole my luminous paint,' Toby shouted.

'I didn't *steal* anything.'

'I don't steal stuff of yours,' Toby went on remorselessly.

26

Roy was distracted from this argument when he noticed Ronnie moving slowly into the room, eyes shut, hands out before her, groping the air like a sleepwalker.

She was, normally, a whimsical woman, with long blonde hair and an oval face that came to a soft, pointed chin. Her eyes were usually wide open, often under brows raised at one of her husband's weird ideas. Now she was moving like a blind person, and a miniature replica of her seemed to be tagging along as a caboose. Three-year-old Sylvia had hold of Ronnie's long skirt and was lifting her feet up high and putting them down ever so slowly, her eyes shut tight, too.

'Ronnie,' Neary started to say.

'Brad,' Ronnie said, ignoring her husband, her eyes still shut, her face expressionless. 'Brad, here's an arithmetic problem for you. If there are seven days in a week and your mother is home all seven of them, how many days are left to your mother?'

He didn't need the calculator. 'Zero!'

'Ronnie,' Neary said again. He didn't like where this was going. 'Open your eyes.'

'Why?' she asked. 'I can walk through the whole house like this. Make the beds, put on the coffee, feed the kids. All without opening my eyes. I'm like Toby's hamster in his cage.'

'No, really,' Roy said. 'Open your eyes. Watch this.'

Ronnie's eyes opened slowly. Humming a tuneless tune that indicated he was pleased with himself, Neary pushed a button on the model railroad's control panel. The children and their mother watched a tiny sailboat stir into motion, gliding

27

across a mirror-like lake. It sailed closer to a rail-road bridge, over which a train was about to roar. But as the train reached the bridge, it stopped.

The drawbridge swiveled sideways on a centre pivot. With tiny tacking movements, the sailboat whirred through the open space, and the draw-bridge started to swivel shut. Without waiting for it to close, the train whipped forward and catapulted neatly into space, crashing down on the lake with a metallic clatter.

Neary's grin disappeared. 'Hmm.'

Ronnie's stare lifted from the train crash to her husband's face. 'Gee, Roy,' she said in a flat tone. 'That was ... really ... great.'

'It worked a while ago.'

'Um-hm.' Her level stare – her eyes were an even fiercer blue than Toby's – never lifted. 'I give this railroad two more weeks,' she said. 'I bet it ends up in the basement with the auto-tennis and the electric toilet and all the rest.'

'That's not fair.'

'Okay, not all,' she granted. 'That worm ranch you had in here. At least you dumped that into the backyard and not down in the cellar.' She picked up the newspaper and started paging through it, look-ing for something, anything. 'Jesus, can't we do something? I'm serving time in this house.'

'We got out last weekend,' Neary offered.

'Walking across the street to the Taylors' is *not* getting out of the house.'

'You get out every day when you take Brad to school,' Neary suggested.

'It's as fully rewarding an experience as when I take Toby to school. Or take Sylvia to the supermarket. Or take the car to get the snow tyres switched for regulars.'

Neary winced inwardly. 'You're painting a very dull picture,' he said.

'Give me a different brush.'

'Listen, if you think my job with the power company is some kind of glamour life . . .' Neary trailed off, wondering how angry she really was. Ronnie had the ability to burn out her anger quickly. 'Listen' he told her, 'when you've fixed one burned-out transformer, you've fixed them all.'

Ronnie stared blankly at him. 'I think it's that new thing they're always talking about,' she said.

'What new thing?'

'Life-style. I think we have to change ours.'

'That's for the rich people, honey,' Roy said. 'They just call up the store and order a whole new life-style.'

'Maybe it isn't life-style,' Ronnie said. 'Maybe it's that other thing the magazines talk about . . . quality of life.'

'Sounds like a soap opera.'

'There has to be more to life than stalking the supermarket aisles looking for three rolls of paper towels for a dollar.'

Neary was silent for a long moment. She had never butted him about how much he earned, or whether they had enough money to live on or not. He'd always assumed they did okay.

'I got a raise in January,' he began cautiously.

She shook her head. 'Wrong track. I'm not talking about money. I don't mind searching for specials in the store. As long as something special

29

is going on somewhere in my life. And, Roy,' she added, 'you know me. I'm easy.'

'Huh?'

'I'm not asking for a week in Acapulco. I mean I'm so starved for something to happen, I'd go bananas if you brought me home a flower. One perfect rose.'

Neary winced again. 'I always forget that.'

'When you crave change the way I do,' Ronnie said, 'you'll settle for anything. New potholders. Going down to the Hertz office and watching them rent Pintos. Calling time and weather and dial-a-joke.'

'Listen,' Toby said, intent on getting back to important things. 'He took my luminous paints.'

Ronnie folded the newspaper to the movie section and stuck it in front of her husband. 'Play through this on your calculator,' she suggested.

Neary glanced down at the page. 'Hey! Guess what? *Pinocchio*'s in town.'

'Who?' Brad asked.

Ronnie had opened her handbag and was examining her face in a compact mirror. 'I smile too much;' she said. 'My mouth is thinning out. The dangerous age.'

'*Pinocchio*,' Neary said. 'You boys have never seen *Pinocchio*. Are you guys in luck!'

Brad frowned. 'You promised Goofy Golf this weekend.'

For once, Toby was in agreement. 'That's right. Goofy Golf.'

'But *Pinocchio* is so great,' Roy said.

'Thinning out,' Ronnie repeated aloud to herself, 'and turning mean. Just like my mother's mouth.'

Brad produced a great sigh. 'Who wants to see some dumb cartoon rated 'G' for kids?'

'How old are you?' his father demanded.

'Eight.'

'Wanna be nine?'

'Yes.'

'We're seeing *Pinocchio* tomorrow,' Neary said.

'Winning your children's hearts and minds,' Ronnie commented to her reflection in the mirror.

'Just kidding,' he told her. 'But I grew up on *Pinocchio*. Kids are still kids, Ronnie. They'll eat it up.' He hummed softly for a moment, then sang a few words. 'When you wish upon a star ... makes no difference – ' Neary stopped. He could see that he wasn't getting through to anybody, neither children nor wife.

'You're right,' he said, throwing up his hands. 'Fellas, you can make up your own minds and I won't influence you in any way. Tomorrow you can play miniature golf which means a lot of waiting in line and pushing and shoving and maybe scoring zero ... or ... you can see *Pinocchio* which has music and animals and magical stuff and things you'll remember for the rest of your lives.'

Then, in desperation: 'Let's vote.'

'Golf!' all three children shouted.

Neary pretended to stagger back. 'Okay, tomorrow, golf. Tonight ... bedtime. Right now. Get going.'

'No, wait,' Toby protested. 'You said we could watch *The Ten Commandments* on TV.'

Across the room the telephone rang. Ronnie moved to answer it. 'That picture is four hours long,' she said, picking up the phone on the second ring. 'Hello. Oh, hi, Earl.'

Neary said, almost to himself, 'I told them they could watch only five of the Commandments.'

'Slow up, Earl,' Ronnie said into the phone. 'I can't relay all that. You better tell Roy direct.' She held out the phone to her husband. 'Something's up.'

Neary started around the ping pong table. 'My kids don't want to see *Pinocchio*,' he grumbled. 'What a world.'

'He'll be there,' Ronnie said into the phone. 'He's crossing the Alps.'

Roy gave her a silent sarcastic 'ha ha' and reached for the phone. Instead of handing it to him, Ronnie held it to his ear with one hand while moving around to snuggle against his other side, kissing his other ear. Neary was used to this sudden mood-switch of hers. He leaned over and picked up Sylvia, who wanted to kiss his ear, too.

'What's the problem, Earl?' he asked his colleague at the power company.

'I got a call from the Load Dispatcher,' Earl Johnson said, his voice high with worry. 'Big drain on the primary voltage.'

'On primary?' Roy said. 'How the hell—?'

'Shut up and listen,' Earl cut in. 'We've lost half a bank of transformers at the Gilmore substation,' he said, trying to get the words out as fast as possible. 'It'll hit the residentials any minute, so put on your pants while you've still got the light.'

'Earl, what the—?'

"Get over to Gilmore fast, Roy.'

The line went dead as Earl hung up. Neary

turned toward his wife. 'Did you hear that—?'

Then the room went dark. Everything stopped dead. In the abrupt darkness, Neary saw them first. Tiny pools of blue light on the model railroad layout where the river went under the bridge and into a small lake. The painted water flowed bluish-green, like Ronnie's eyes.

'I told you!' Toby howled suddenly. 'I told you! He stole my luminous paint.'

FIVE

A Moog synthesizer is nothing if not complicated. There are still not many of them in the world, and still fewer people who know how to put one together, and even fewer who understand what to do with the thing: its capabilities, its potential, its limits.

Therefore, when the rush order came through to modify the synthesizer they had constructed for Stevie Wonder two years before, the bearded, moustached and bespectacled young men who understand these arcane matters proceeded with bemused diligence.

Bemused because, evidently, Mr. Wonder was lending or giving his Moog to a group not previously known for their musical interests. But what the hell? What could these guys do with a Moog synthesizer that they couldn't already do with a nuclear-tipped long-range intercontinental ballistic missile?

SIX

Ike Harris was holding on to two telephones when Roy arrived: one connected directly to an apartment elevator in which Supervisor Grimsby was trapped, the other to the equally-agitated outside world.

Harris was shaken. 'A 27-KV line at Gilmore went,' he said into the phone at Grimsby; at the same time, he was briefing Neary. 'All the breakers opened and we started losing feeders. Tolono's dark. Crystal Lake's dark. What? Oh, that's right, sir. You're dark, too.' Harris glanced at Neary and his eyes went up in his head for a moment, signalling the kind of vibes Grimsby was transmitting at his end.

'Okay, right,' Ike said, when Grimsby was temporarily through screaming. 'I've got reports of vandalism on the line. Some 890-megawatt lines seem to be down all over. I called Municipal Lighting for a fix, but we can't send the new juice through till this 500-KV tower is operational. What? Yes, sir!'

Harris put his hand over the phone. 'Neary, you know the normal wire tension in that area?'

'Without wind, normal tension for the sag is about fifteen thousand pounds per wire. I was a journeyman out that way a couple of years ago.'

Ike took his hand away from the phone. 'I'm sending Neary over there now.'

'You are?' Roy mouthed.

Harris waved Neary out of the control room with the hand not holding the Grimsby-phone. 'Get the hell going. On the double. No, not you, Mr. Grimsby.'

As Roy started trotting out the door, he heard Ike shouting to someone, everyone, anyone. 'Tell Municipal we're going to candle power in ten minutes.'

Now, fifteen minutes later, barrel-assing down a dark county road whose name or number he wasn't sure about, Neary was about to admit to being lost. Roy's car was a smaller version of his workroom at home. He had a network map spread out over the steering wheel as he searched vainly for the problem coordinates, a pen light sticking out of his mouth.

Already a menace on the road, Neary was further distracted by the police calls that were squabbling over his broad band radio.

'This is Sheriff's Dispatch. Do I have a patrol car near Reva Road?'

'Hello, County. This is highway patrol six-ten. We're on Reva. Can we help you boys out?'

'If you would, thank you. See the woman two-eleven Reva Road. Something about the outdoor lighting. She's in a state. Barking dogs. Go figure it out.'

The radio stopped talking and Neary stopped driving, pulling over to the side of the road. Reva Road was in Tolono, he was sure of it. But Ike had reported Tolono dark. Roy picked up the mobile phone.

'TR eighty-eight eighteen to Trouble Foreman,' he called.

'Here's Trouble,' Ike Harris came back, no less hysterical than fifteen minutes ago. 'What d'ya want?'

'Have you guys restored power to Tolono? Over.'

'Are you kidding? Tolono was the first to go.'

'I just heard the police reporting lights in Tolono.'

'Jesus!' Harris shouted. 'What are you, monitoring police calls on a night like this? Everything's down, Neary. The whole network's fallen.'

Harris went off abruptly.

Neary pulled back onto the road. Several minutes later, he saw a revolving amber light in the distance, which made him feel a little better. But not much. At least he wasn't lost. Roy pulled over behind a utility trouble wagon and got out. Two crews were there, standing by, waiting for someone in authority to give the word. A yellow DWP cherry picker idled, ready to lift men to the top of the tower that loomed indistinctly high in the darkness.

Neary felt inadequate. He'd never bossed line crews before. These guys were good old-timers, most of them. Roy had put in his time on line crews himself but these guys were fifteen years older than he was and ten times as experienced. Just because he'd moved up through the system didn't mean a damn thing to these fellows, didn't automatically mean they'd follow his orders, if he could think of any orders to give.

Then Roy picked out a friendly face, a black one, Earl Johnson, who'd called him earlier.

'Hi, Earl,' Neary said. 'What's up?'

'Down,' said Earl, white teeth grinning in the revolving amber light. 'Why do you think somebody would steal two miles of transmission wire?'

'You're kidding.'

By way of answer, Earl lifted his six-volt flashlight and aimed its beam to the top of the tower. Then he traced a line where two thick copper wires should have sagged along to the next tower. But there were no wires.

'The line's not down,' he said. 'It's gone. There's nothing from M-Ten to M-Twelve.'

'I'll be damned,' Neary said. 'Maybe it's the high price of copper,' he mused.

Earl and Roy started back to Neary's car to report.

'Right,' Earl said. 'Right. Stuff's worth a fortune. I told them we ought to lay power cable underground.'

'But where would the birds land?' Neary said.

Before Roy could report to Ike Harris, the radio flashed a police call. 'To any unit in the vicinity of Tolono foothills ... a housewife reports ... uh ... her Tiffany lamp flashing in the kitchen window ... upside-down lamp ...'

'Where'd he say?' Johnson asked. 'Tolono?'

'That's the second report from Tolono,' Neary told him.

'Can't make it out clearly,' the police dispatcher came through again. 'Very distraught ... four-one-five-five Osborne Road.'

'But Tolono's dark,' Earl said.

'Maybe,' Roy said, picking up the car phone. 'TR eighty-eight eighteen. Let me talk to Ike.' He handed Earl the map. 'Find Osborne, will you?' he asked. 'I never could read these damn things.'

Harris came on. 'Neary! What's happening?'

'Well,' said Roy conversationally, 'I'm here at Maryten. And ... all the lines have been swiped. All the way to Mary-twelve, Earl here says. It looks like vandals made a very sloppy cut at the terminals, then backed a truck in and pulled out all the grounds, but here's something else—'

'Here's something for you,' Ike cut in. 'We've got to pick up the system in one hour.'

'One hour!' Neary exclaimed. 'It's a mile of empty poles out here. That's impossible.'

'Anything's possible when you've got a general supervisor stuck in an elevator who wants out.'

Roy gave Ike a small laugh, then asked, 'Say, Ike? You haven't restored power to Tolono, have you?'

'I told you, Tolono was the first to go. It's as dark as the inside of Grimsby's elevator.'

'Now look, Ike,' Neary began in a careful tone. 'Hear me out. The police are reporting lights in Tolono. If the lines out there are energized and it's not showing up on your data bank, one of your people working high around those terminals — ga-zaap! It happened in Gilroy once. Remember?'

'Me and two backup computers say Tolono's as dark as the inside of your head, Neary,' Harris shouted.

Earl Johnson affected not to have heard this slur.

'See the complainants at Tolono South Reservoir,' the police dispatcher suddenly called. 'Christmas lights have started a minor brush fire.'

'Did you hear that? They're saying Christmas lights now.'

'This is May, not December,' Harris said, suddenly his old cheerful self. 'There is no Christmas

41

during a blackout. Only Hallowe'en.' And he hung up before Roy could respond.

Neary turned to Earl Johnson. 'What's wrong with that guy? This is how Jordie Christopher bought it, replacing shot-out insulators in Gilroy.'

'You heard the man, Roy,' Earl said. 'He told you to fix the line.'

'Right.'

Neary stood there, humming softly for a moment. Then he turned back to Earl Johnson and said conspiratorially to him, 'Say, Earl, how'd you like to sign on this operation for about an hour?'

He was climbing in the car, closing the door and starting the engine before Johnson began to respond.

'Me? Run this show? Who's gonna listen to me? I'm not even seniority. I'm not even white. Don't turn your back on a good thing, Roy. They made you boss cow.'

'Earl, if he's wrong, some of our Tolono people could get killed.'

'If he's right, they'll suspend your ass so high even the job placement corps won't find it.'

Neary started easing the car forward. 'Tolono is what?' he asked out the window. 'Sixty-six alternate to seventy?'

Roy drove away.

Johnson held his head in agony over Neary and his sense of direction. 'You gonna wind up in Cincinnati,' he yelled after him. 'It's seventy to sixty-six.'

Neary waved back at Johnson. Seventy to sixty-six.

A moment later, the night swallowed up the shape and sound of his car.

Earl Johnson watched the tail lights grow dim and then disappear. He heaved a heavy sigh and walked slowly back to the gang of linemen, watching him with a mixture of suspicion and amused malice.

Earl stood there before the veteran repairmen, wondering what on earth to tell them to do. He took a deep breath and pointed toward the tower overhead. 'Fix it.'

SEVEN

Aireast Flight 31 touched down on the tarmac at
11:40 p.m. The Indianapolis Airport tower issued
routine taxi instructions to the A.E. Concourse; a
short three minute dogleg from the East-West
runway.

A brace of airport security police waited curb-
side, their walkie-talkies gargling squelch while a
futzed voice told the public that the white zones
were for the immediate unloading of passengers
only.

A black Ford L.T.D. carved a trail through the
mild late night congestion, smoking its tyres inches
away from the fleet of the airport security patrol.
One tyre actually lurched up over the white curb-
side with enough noise and danger to make any cop
grab for his citation pad.

Instead, one of the security officers reached for
the rear door and held it open. Three men got out.
Were they pro football players disguised as Sperry-
Rand accounting executives? Their Brooks
Brothers pinstripes looked as if they had been
ironed right onto their six foot sinewy frames. Two
of the men wore sunglasses and the other had a
grey moustache that didn't quite match his short
blond hair.

A fourth C.P.A. type, nearly resembling Fran
Tarkenton, came running, out of breath, through
the electric terminal doors.

'It's down!'

'When?'

'Just about a minute ago. Where have you been? She's on the taxi to Gate 55A.'

The front four began to run into the terminal annex, shouldering open the electric doors when they wouldn't move fast enough.

They charged the Up escalator, taking it two steps at a time. At the top, the first of them bounced off a woman who did not see them coming, and the other three almost piled into them. Instead, they dodged around their colleague and the woman, who was somewhat pregnant and was sprawled on the floor, and took off.

The first man picked up the pregnant lady, with many apologies, ascertained that she was all right, startled but otherwise okay, and took off after his friends. She remembered a small plastic card with his face on it, dangling from a thin metal chain around his neck.

The first man caught up with his colleagues trotting through the security metal detectors. They all waved their badges on their little chains at the security personnel and were waved through. Now they started sprinting down the long corridor leading to the arrival-departure gates, as if to make up for lost time.

But instead of running down to any of the gates, they suddenly skidded to a stop in front of a door marked only by a small number '6', someone remembered later, and, without knocking, charged in.

Seconds later, the front four re-emerged, bringing with them three very bewildered F.A.A. officials. They donned plastic photo IDs but had no resemblance to pro-ball players. They were as C.P.A. as they come. And angry and getting angrier as the hastily-assembled group crowded around the airport tower entrance, fumbling in pockets for a pass key.

Aireast 31, a 727, had stopped for thirty seconds, waiting out some surface traffic. Now she was moving again, heading right for the docking area 55A. Suddenly 31 hit its brakes and lurched once before stopping. The nose wheel began to shift hard to starboard.

Guiding the aircraft to the concourse was a ground attendant, his flashsticks frozen above his head. The jet continued to starboard. Anxiously, the ground attendant waved his flashsticks. 'This way, over here!'

A.E. 31, totally ignoring the signal, pivoted full around and headed for a private section of runway, with blue flashing dead-end lights.

Helplessly, the attendant let his sticks sag, then shrugged over toward the baggage boys who were peering up at the control tower for signs of life.

Meanwhile, in another part of the airport – unaware of the unseemly hullabaloo taking place – Lacombe, the proximate cause of it all, landed. His military jet taxied off a main runway to a little-used parking area and stopped next to a black Cadillac limousine. The twin jet engines screamed to a stop, the door opened, and the slight Frenchman stepped quickly, but not hurriedly, down the metal steps, across the concrete and into the back seats of the Cadillac.

In the front seat of the limousine were a Government driver in military dress and another man dressed in a business suit. Lacombe, in his austere, controlled manner, waved aside all preliminaries about his trip, etc., and asked, 'They are prepared?'

'Yes, sir,' said the man in the business suit.

The driver moved the limousine further away from the passenger terminal to an area where freight was stored for trans-shipment. There were four other cars already parked there, motors running, headlights off. As the Cadillac pulled up in front of the others, one car door opened and a young man emerged and trotted over.

He leaned in the front window next to the driver, and said, 'Monsieur Lacombe?'

'*Oui, c'est moi,*' the man in the back seat responded.

'I'm your translator.'

'*Bon. Entrez s'il vous plaît.*'

The young man opened a back door and got in.

Lacombe started searching his pockets. 'You are . . .' He fished out a scrap of paper and read it in the dim ceiling light, trying to pronounce what he saw in phonetic English. 'Mees-ter Lay-oog-line?'

'Laughlin. David.'

Lacombe shrugged, almost bitter at his lack of English, and pulled out of another pocket a paperback book. 'And you are on the project . . . two years?'

'At the Wright-Patterson Facility, Dayton, Ohio,' Laughlin said. 'I had the privilege,' he went on enthusiastically, 'of working for your executive assistant in seventy-one. Transcribed twenty-one hours of sleep-tape and attended the Montsoreau talks the week the French broke through. Congratulations, again, by the way.'

'Thank you,' Lacombe said, apparently unmoved by either Laughlin's experience or enthusiasm. 'Translate, please.'

To David Laughlin's confusion and embarrassment, Lacombe began reading the paperback aloud in French. It was something quite passionate and he varied his inflections and emotions as, evidently, the occasion demanded.

Laughlin translated, a syllable or so behind him. He was very good at it, but he wondered just what the hell was going on here. He had heard – everyone connected with the project had heard – that Lacombe was . . . interesting. After all, he had been through four interpreters already in the last nine months.

'Her firm young breasts heaved with excitement as she slipped off her woolly sweater,' David translated.

'Her nipples were as hard, pink, and round as bubble-gum,' Laughlin went on. By this time, he was sweating like mad in the cool night air, and shouting to be heard over the noise of the taxiing jet. 'She squealed with excitement as her teacher slowly pulled out a long, stiff ruler.'

'Fine . . . Fine,' Lacombe shouted, stopping.

The jet engines whined down.

Laughlin was relieved. He looked hard at the slight man, whose face was lined with fatigue and whose sharp, black eyes studied Laughlin as closely as he was being fixed, as if trying to search out some signs of intelligence in that young, very-American face that was apparently untouched by experience or pain.

'If I may ask, sir,' Laughlin broke the spell

awkwardly, 'why that particular book?'

Lacombe shrugged and showed David the front of the paperback, with its vivid cover and French title, 'The Cloak Room'. 'Something I buy,' he said wearily. 'I am sure it have emotional value. Emotions are going to be important, Lay-oog-line. There is equivalents . . . emotional and linguistic, in every language. I expect these word equivalents. I want to be understood perfectly.' The Frenchman leaned forward and said to the man in the front seat, 'Robert, how was he?'

'Hot damn!' the man said.

It was the only time Laughlin ever heard him speak.

Lacombe looked confused until David jumped in and supplied the idiomatic French for 'hot damn'.

Thus concluded David Laughlin's job interview. Lacombe smiled, shook his hand and opened the car door all at the same time. He set out for the 727 and Laughlin scrambled after him.

Inside Aireast 31, the wilted passengers – too tired to complain any more and too relieved to have landed in Indianapolis at long last – watched bleary-eyed as the forward door was opened by a stewardess and six large men crowded up the movable stairs that had been pushed up to the side of the plane, through the hatch and into the compartment. Two of the men, in business suits, disappeared into the flight crew's cabin while the other four – dressed in unmatching slacks, ties and jackets, their plastic badges dangling over their ties – stood by the open door and in the aisle, as though to block any exit.

By this time all forty-four passengers had become more curious than tired, when the next thing they saw was their pilot, co-pilot, radio man and flight engineer leaving the cockpit under the escort of the two men in business suits. Those passengers able to look out the starboard windows watched their flight crew get into two waiting automobiles and be driven away. The men in suits came back up the stairs and into the plane again.

Two of the unmatching men now started moving down the aisle, handing out little pencils and small IBM cards. As they did this, one of the men in suits asked a stewardess for the cabin microphone. She gave it to him. He pushed the speaker button, speaking in the false, friendly tones of a public relations man.

'Folks,' he said, 'I'm Jack DeForest, speaking to you on behalf of Air Force Research and Development Command, apologising for the delay in your flight and personal schedules. We really want to get you all on your way just as soon as possible.

'Okay,' he went on like a shipboard social director. 'This is nobody's fault, but during your flight, unknown to your pilot or Aireast Airlines, your aircraft accidentally passed through a restricted corridor where classified government testing was being conducted.'

That got a reaction from the passengers: a series of grunts and muttered 'I thought so's'.

'Now, I said this wouldn't take long and it won't,' Jack DeForest went on. 'I'm going to ask all passengers with cameras, exposed film canisters, boxes of unexposed film and tape recording devices to turn them over to our courtesy team at this time.'

Now the reaction was instant and angry. Jack held up a hand, which no one could see except the stewardess. 'Just temporarily, folks. You'll have them all back within two weeks. That's a promise. You fill in those little cards we handed out with your name, address, and a description of whatever you're turning over to the Air Force. And you will definitely get it all back . . . slides, prints, whatever . . . at our expense.'

Jack DeForest let the complaining run its course. Behind him, Lacombe entered the aircraft, Laughlin at his shoulder. They all watched the passengers, still grumbling, begin filling in the IBM cards.

Lacombe turned sideways to Laughlin and whispered something to him in French.

'Mr. DeForest,' Laughlin said, at which point the eyes of every passenger raised up to see what was going to happen now. 'Tell the flight crew we need the flight recorder intact. And one thing more.'

'Yes.'

'Don't wash the plane.'

Laughlin had snapped out Lacombe's whispered orders without thinking of anything more than translating them into English. Now, as he watched the passengers' frightened and concerned reactions, David realised it would have been smarter to have talked to the flight crew personally himself.

The passengers' faces reflected exactly what nobody wanted them to reflect. It had been the business of not washing the plane.

It was a bad moment. But no one spoke. Perhaps they were too tired. Perhaps they didn't really want to know. Perhaps they'd just had enough for one day.

Lacombe, Laughlin, DeForest and the others knew that at least a couple of the passengers would start searching out the press the next day. But they felt sure that the only accounts of the experience that would ever get into print would appear in the pages of *The Enquirer, The Star, Argosy* and other periodicals that no one of any consequence took seriously. Still, Lacombe, Laughlin, DeForest and the others knew that there was no way to stop what was happening that night. It was only the beginning.

EIGHT

There was no way the dispatcher could get to Neary. He'd switched off the mobile phone unit in his car. Roy didn't want Ike Harris calling him. As he drove through the night to Tolono, he could see a blanket of stars above him, although the usual spring night ground fog was rising out of the gullies, bouncing his headlights back at him.

Neary did not ride alone. He had the police calls for company.

'U-five. Officer Longly. Over.'

'Go ahead.'

'Responding to the 10–75 on Cornbread Road and Middletown Pike. I am observing . . . I think it's street lights in the foothill residentials. We're on our way.'

A bright group of high beams appeared over Neary's shoulder out the back window. He was tearing at his maps and absently waved his arm out the side window. The automobile headlights passed him, and somebody shouted out the car, 'You're in the middle of the road, jerkwater!'

'Couple of hundred neighbours in their pajamas think it's Saturday night out here,' Longly observed on the police band.

Neary spread a map over the steering wheel, finally locating Cornbread and Middletown. D-five, M-thirty-four. He took off, tyres screeching.

Within five minutes, Neary was hopelessly lost. Finally, in utter desperation, he pulled into a row of darkened fast food franchises. The blackout had, apparently, provided a perfect excuse for everyone to hang out in the parking areas. As soon as a bunch of them saw Neary's DWP truck, they crowded about him, waving flashlights and cans of Coors.

'Did your lights come back on?' he asked them.

'You asking us?' a lady in curlers and kerchief asked. 'What do you do for a living?'

'What about the street lights? When they went off did they come on? On off, on off.'

A wise-ass kid stuck a flashlight in Roy's face. 'Like this?' he said, blinking the light blindingly on and off, on and off in Neary's eyes.

'Yes.'

'No,' the kid said, laughing cretinously.

'Am I in Tolono or where?' Neary asked Mrs. Curlers.

'It's all lit up out here,' Officer Longly said suddenly. 'These street lamps ... I think sodium vapor. Don't want to stay still. They're revolving in some draft. They go up ... they go down ... wait one ... they also want to go a little sideways.'

'Jesus!' Neary said.

'Longly,' the dispatcher said, sounding bored. 'Give us a location.'

'Give me one, too,' said Neary.

'It's over the Ingleside Elementary School heading northeast.'

Roy yelled out the window, 'Where's the Ingleside Elementary School ... Anybody?'

'That's easy,' said a guy, who was carrying a shotgun for some reason. 'You go back to 70 then—'

'No, wait a sec,' Longly called. 'Heading North-west on Daytona.'

'Where's Daytona? Quick!'

'That's even easier.' The gunslinger was seeing action now. 'Okay, Jack, take any road out east of here till you get to city-nine and farm-eleven, but don't stop there 'cause there's a detour sign:

'Pardon Our Progress'.

He was still going on as Neary shifted gears and backed away.

Five minutes later, Neary was lost in his own home town. He was on some country road, sur-rounded by more of that stupid ground fog. Bump-ing over a rutted crossroads, the DWP truck stopped and Roy Neary shone his spotlight at a street sign. Shit! he checked the map again. *Shit!* Neary scooped out two troughs of Indiana clay as he ground the gears backwards, stopped again and spread the map over the steering wheel, twisting the little gooseneck lamp into bright submission.

Behind him a bank of lights from an approaching vehicle lit up the rear window. They drew right up behind Neary and stopped. The glare, bouncing off his rear and side view mirrors, was almost as irri-tating as that municipal map with all of its myopic lines. Absently, he stuck his hand out his left hand window and waved the other vehicle around him.

For a moment, nothing happened. The intense light, as if from a semi-truck's double-beams, now stung his eyes. Impatiently now, he waved them around again.

Without a sound, moving at a slow, hypnotic pace, the super highbeams complied . . . rising *vertically* out of sight, leaving darkness behind.

Intent on the map, Roy Neary had seen none of this. His subconscious registered vaguely that the bright lights were no longer bothering him. What finally penetrated his consciousness was this noise. It sounded like the rattling of tin. Neary looked up, then around, and finally shone his spotlight on the road sign.

It was vibrating so fast that the letters seemed to multiply and superimpose. He looked again, making unknowingly a 'Huuuh?' sound. Next, the truck's spotlight, dashboard lamp and headlights faded to a faint amber glow and then went out.

Abruptly, the entire area for thirty yards around him was assaulted by a silent explosion of the brightest light imaginable. It was suddenly daytime. Neary tried to look out his open window, but the light was too bright and he had to duck back in. He felt an immediate burning, followed by a prickling sensation on the side of his face that he had been unwise enough to stick out the window. Neary went for the phone, but it was dead. The broad band radio had crackled out, too.

By now, Roy was too frightened to budge. Just his eyes moved. Then he threw his hands over his eyes and groped for his metal-rimmed sunglasses clipped to the visor above the windshield. He managed to get them on, and then – to his horror – found they were buzzing at his temples, vibrating as intensely as the road sign.

That was when the glove compartment, falling open at the hinges, began to rattle violently as everything metallic started sticking together. A box of paper clips popped open and dozens of the damn things flew past Neary's head and fastened themselves to the roof of the truck.

The sunglasses were too hot. They were burning his skin. Neary whipped them off his face and let them drop to the seat. Instead, they, too, flew past his head and stuck to the roof. He closed his eyes against the fierce light. The ashtray emptied itself out as though sucked weightless by a current of air from outside the truck and ...

The hot light was gone. Paper clips rained down on Roy's head. He could no longer hear the sign shaking. He looked up and – for a second – saw the stars. Then, as if some tremendous tray was sliding out overhead, all the stars (except a few around the edges) were inked out by the limbo shape. Fluidly, the mass moved on and the stars started coming back out.

A distant rattling caused Neary to bring his head back inside and swing around in his seat. Suddenly his highbeams, spot and lamp switched back on. Down the road there was a four-way stop. All four signs were dancing to and fro, vibrating so violently that metal around the sign's edges curled against the force. For a second, the intersection was awash in that same blinding light. But for only a second. And in the dark, the signs were no longer vibrating.

All was still. Not even the hint of a breeze.

And then the radio blasted on, and Neary screamed.

It was making noises that sounded like electrical overload, and the voices weren't much better as far as Roy was concerned.

'I don't know. I'm asking *you*. Is there a full moon tonight?'

'That's a negative,' the dispatcher, a female voice, said. 'New moon on the thirteenth.'

'Get out of here. Me and my partner are seeing this thing over Signal Hill. This is the thing everybody is screaming about. It's the moon . . .' There was a lot of static. 'Wait a sec. Okay. It's starting to move now. West to East.'

'This is Tolono,' a new voice came on. 'Police ten-eleven. We are watching it, confirming it is definitely the moon. Be advised it is not moving. The clouds behind it are moving, giving it the illusion of movement over—'

'Where'd you study astronomy, Tolono?' a voice that Roy recognised as Longly's broke in. 'When did you ever see clouds moving *behind* the moon?'

'What's your location?' the lady dispatcher asked wearily.

'Just off the Telemar Expressway and east toward Harper Valley.'

'Oh, my God!' Roy Neary cried. 'I know where that is.'

Neary hit ninety-plus. He found himself entering a long, dark tunnel and as his high headlights cut through it, Roy became aware again of the prickling sensation on the side of his face. He also remembered how frightened he had been back there, and here he was now chasing after the thing that had so scared him. He really ought to stop, turn around and go back to Earl and the other guys. But, Neary realised, he was more excited than frightened now. He felt like a kid. It was too late to stop now. He was having too much fun. And so were the police.

'I see them, Charlie! I'm in pursuit.'

'You can take it for what it's worth. These things were not manufactured in Detroit.' That was Longly!

'It's decelerating. I don't know why it's decelerating, but it's getting closer. Three hundred yards.'

'Can you catch up to it?' the dispatcher asked.

'I don't think so. About two hundred yards. That's it for me. I don't think we should rush into it.'

'It's following all the S-turns. It's following all the roads.'

'Radar shows 'em down to twenty-five miles per hour.'

'Hey, wasn't that a school zone we just passed through?'

'Look at the traffic lights! They turn to green just as they get up to them.'

A lot of static.

'Yes, sir ... They're going right out east on Harper Valley.'

Neary came out of the tunnel and rounded a curve at ninety-five miles an hour, traded paint with a guard rail, went into a skid and managed to correct without running off into the central divider gully. He shot past a sign: East Harper Valley Exit – 3 miles. Then Neary really stood on the accelerator, slowing to eighty-five when the Harper Valley exit loomed up.

Skidding and braking, he whipped the truck off onto the exit road. It turned into a two-lane country road and Roy came down to a more cautious seventy.

Up ahead he thought he might have seen something on the ...

A child!

Neary stood on the brakes. An instant later, a woman ran out onto the road and grabbed for the child. The truck was skidding wildly now as Roy fought the wheel. The woman and child were frozen in his headlights for another instant – yards, feet ahead, directly under the wheels.

Neary threw the wheel hard left, skidded by the two bodies and plowed into a snow fence, taking some of it with him before coming to rest.

For a long moment, everything was very still except for his panting breath. He switched off the engine. It took him three tries to get the door handle to work, so shaky were his arm muscles.

Neary finally staggered out of the high weeds back to the centre of the road. The woman stared blindly at him, her arms around the little boy, her hands over the boy's eyes, as if still shutting away from him the high, bright headlights bearing down upon them.

'Lady,' Roy began, 'you shouldn't let your little boy—'

'I've been searching for him for hours,' Jillian Guiler burst out. 'He wandered away from our house. I've been looking for hours. He just ran away. Hours and hours I've been—'

'Okay,' Neary said. 'Okay, I'm sorry I—'

'That's a dangerous curve,' a voice said.

Neary turned to see – of all things – an old farmer sitting in a chair on the back of an ancient pickup. His family, a wife and two sons, were grouped around him, some with binoculars, one boy with a toy telescope.

'Just like the circus coming to town,' the farmer

was saying, taking a swig from a bottle of something. 'They come through at night . . . they come through late so they don't disturb the residents.'

A sudden wind sent Jillian's hair flying back from her face. Roy could feel his own hair blown in the same direction. He turned to face the wind, whistling now through the snow fence.

In Neary's truck, tangled in yards of torn-up snow fence, the police radio talked on.

'Can you run a make on them?'

'. . . I may be gaining again.'

'As long as they keep following the road.'

'This is Randolf County. We're monitoring you on the emergency frequency. What've you guys got down there?'

Squinting downwind, Neary could see something coming along the road, but it turned out to be a low-winging flight of birds, escaping something. Something on the horizon. Something that glowed.

A group of rabbits bounded past, ears flat against their heads.

'Here they come again,' the farmer said.

Neary whirled back to stare down the road.

'Jesus!' he whispered to himself. 'Jesus Chr—'

The very breath seemed to have been sucked out of his lungs. The vacuum was filled by a low bass rumble, as though the air was being disturbed by lightning. Closing soundlessly upon them at high speed was what looked like a brace of kleig lights supported on something large. Neary had the impression of a shape behind the light, something solid, nuts and bolts. It was like a sudden sunrise at two a.m., flying past him from east to west.

Without thinking, Roy covered his face with one arm and grabbed for the woman and the boy with the other. Jillian felt her face and neck burn, then prickle. The three clung tightly together as something like an Indian-summer sunset, flashing and blinking autumn colours, swept past them, slowing above the road ahead. A billboard featuring McDonald's Golden Arches was studded by six shades of light, before the massive Christmas ornament moved on, a white spot picking out the dotted line on the road beneath it.

A third vehicle – resembling a jack-o'-lantern to Neary because there almost seemed to be a phantom face leering out of all the bright lights, out of all the thousands of little stained-glass coloured sections – closed over, then past them and, following the road, made a right turn, signalled by three sequential directional lights flashing red like a '71 Cougar.

Neary and Jillian were gasping with fright, but little Barry was jumping up and down, shouting, 'Ice cream! Ice cream!' and laughing. He was very excited.

The old farmer, still sitting in his chair in the back of the pickup, said casually, 'Yep, they can fly rings around the moon, but we're years ahead of 'em on the highway.'

That was too much for Roy and Jillian. Their eyes locked, but they could think of nothing to say.

Neary swallowed, trying to get some words, some sounds, something out of his mouth. Something more was coming down the road. With a desperate shove he threw himself, Jillian and Barry off to the side of the road.

Just in time. Two police cruisers howled past at well over one hundred-and-twenty miles per hour.

Neary headed back for his truck.

'Stick around,' the farmer said to him. 'You should've seen it an hour ago.'

'This is nuts,' said Neary, just as another Indiana cruiser roared by.

'I may be drunk but I know I'm here,' the old man shouted over the roar.

Neary was upset. 'You nearly killed us!' he yelled after the last cruiser.

Barry was laughing again.

Neary started backing the truck out of the tangle of snow fencing and high weeds. He spun his wheels in frustration, then calmed down and got the truck out of there.

'Where are we?' Neary asked Jillian.

'Harper Valley.'

The truck took off.

'They just play,' Barry said, snuggling up against his mother.

'What, Barry?'

'They play nice.'

NINE

Accelerator jammed on the floor, Neary hunched close to the windshield, following the curves of the on-ramp and the glow ahead and above.

As he shot onto the highway, he heard the police calling to each other, although he did not yet have them in sight.

'I'm gaining on them, Bob!'

'Look at them take that curve!'

Roy's head was almost touching the glass. He moved back a moment and glanced down at the speedometer. Ninety-five, ninety-seven, ninety-nine.

'. . . that's the Ohio tolls up there!'

'At these speeds who can see lines!'

Up ahead the flashing red and yellow lights of the last of the cruisers came into Neary's view. He had to slow slightly to hold onto the road as they swept around long bends. The formation of brilliant lights was still far ahead, sweeping smoothly around the bends as if gravity was some abstract theory.

In the distance, the line of toll booths looked deserted to Neary. The normal bluish flourescent lighting apparently blacked out here by the power failure, too. At this hour of the night, there was little traffic between Indiana and Ohio.

At the toll booths, one of the attendants was dozing on his stool. The three flaming orbs soared smoothly up and over the line of booths. All hell broke loose. Red battery-operated alarm lights flashed on and off. Sirens tore the stillness to pieces.

The dozing attendant jerked awake. Some dude was trying to get through his tolls without paying! In the blink of an eye, the first police cruiser shot through the gates. The second cruiser whoosed past, sirens and roof lights crazy. As the attendant started out of the booth to see what the hell, the third cruiser displaced air, followed closely by Neary's yellow DWP truck.

'I'm closing the gap,' one of the policeman called.

'Man, you gotta see this. They're glued to the road!' A hairpin curve was just ahead, and for the first time since the pursuit began the objects decided not to stay glued to the road. They shot straight out over the guardrail and into the air. An instant later, the police officer, obviously locked in on the night lights and doing at least eighty-five, followed them through the guard rail and high into Ohio airspace for a sensational moment before it pancaked into the embankment and lost all of its wheels and doors.

'DeWitt! You O.K., DeWitt?'

The second patrol car seized the opportunity to save itself and, brakes on fire, sideslipped right up to the littered cliffside. Roy saw the two police officers jump over the mangled guard rail and tear down the embankment to the creamed cruiser.

The third police car and then Neary finally stopped. The other cops ran down the embankment, while Neary looked up at the sky. The three firelights arced upward into a low-lying cloud bank. Once inside they turned the clouds to fire until the internal illumination gently faded restoring normal night again. Neary turned back toward Indiana. The flourescent lighting on both sides of the toll booths was flickering back to life. Then Roy saw on the horizon a tapestry of light. A distant city was coming back on. Tolono? Harper Valley? It seemed the blackout was over.

As it turned out, Trooper Roger DeWitt was in better shape than his wrinkled cruiser. Sporting a broken nose, minor but multiple contusions and a possible concussion. He had strutted around the stationhouse for one hour telling everybody including D.W.I.'s, one male rape victim, and a dozen witnesses of that evening's skyjinks his version of God's truth. Now he was inside making his verbal report to Captain Rasmussen while in the State Highway Patrol processing room the other officers and Roy Neary were working up reports of their night to remember. It was now three-thirty a.m., and Neary was fading. A man only has so many ounces of adrenalin, Neary thought. He craved a Mars bar but would have settled for Mounds or M&M's. There weren't enough typewriters to go round, so Roy worked in pencil. He had a landslide of a headache.

'Got any aspirin?' he asked the room.

No one paid any attention to him.

'If Longly hadn't been with me,' one of the troopers said to another, 'I would have gone psychiatric.'

Longly grinned. 'I don't want to file this report,' he said. 'I want to publish it.'

Just then, a door across the room burst open and DeWitt emerged, limping, from the captain's office, closing the door behind him, but not before the Captain shoved through it. 'It's enough to outrage common sense,' the Captain addressed everyone in the processing room. 'Ordinary people look to the police *not* to make bizarre reports of this nature.'

'My knowledge is God's truth,' DeWitt offered in his own defence.

'I will not see this department pressed between the pages of the *National Enquirer*.' Rasmussen looked at Longly and another trooper behind their typewriters. Again he spoke to the room. 'When Flash Gordon and Buck Rogers are done, have them get their behinds in here.'

Slamming back from whence the room fell stone quiet.

'Was he mad 'cause your car's gonna be a taxi next week?'

'Sweet Jesus.' DeWitt now looked dazed as well as damaged. 'I told him the whole thing. I didn't hold back nothing. The shooting stars. The speed. What the hell, I ain't no demolition derby . . . not on purpose.'

'And?'

'He gave me a two week suspension.'

'What?' All the other troopers stopped what they were doing and stared at the man.

'That's what I said.' DeWitt started limping for the door. 'Go try to tell somebody the truth and we'll all be watching daytime TV.'

Roy watched the officers turn to their typewriters. He watched them reading over their respective reports. Some cops exchanged forced smiles. Then, as if some invisible puppeteer pulled simultaneously on five strings, five right hands reached into five typewriters and yanked out from them five n217 forms.

'Go ahead, talk mister,' one officer said to Roy,

smiling sheepishly as he inserted a new report form in his typewriter. 'Be my guest.'

Neary searched for a friend in the room and immediately understood the general situation. He got up and left.

TEN

It was after four by the time Neary got home. From somewhere he had inhaled a new burst of energy while charging down the hall to the bedroom, crying 'Ronnie! Ronnie!' Neary couldn't control himself, every muscle was vibrating from an unforeseen reserve of adrenalin. He was nauseous from all the excitement and his second word almost blew Ronnie out of bed.

'Honey, wake up.'

Her two blue eyes filled with terror, her long blonde hair sprang tangled with sleep.

'What's it, kids . . . and fire wh . . .?'

'It's okay, kids are okay,' he said again. 'Honey, you won't believe this.'

Ronnie caught her breath and stared at the luminous clock dial. 'Right. I don't believe you're waking me up at ten minutes after four.'

'You're not going to believe what's happening.'

'I'm not listening,' Ronnie said distinctly, and pulled the covers over her head.

'You don't have to listen,' Roy's breathing reminded Ronnie of the way little Toby would wolf down dessert. 'They don't make any noise at all. There was nothing but air and all of a sudden whoosh . . . then whoosh . . . then a little red whoosh . . . Jesus!'

From under the covers Ronnie absorbed the whooshes before remembering. 'The Department's been trying to reach you but couldn't reach you . . .'

'Yeah, I know. I shut my phone off.'

She started to wake up. 'Roy, you shouldn't do that. They have to talk to you . . . all kinds of crazy things are going on. The phone has been ringing off the hook. I remember now. They want you to call them now!'

Neary saw that words weren't enough so he used two hands to pull his wife out of bed.

'Come on! Get outta bed. What do you want to wear, dammit. The sun's gonna put the stars out.'

'Roy! What are you talking about.'

'Nothing. I'm not talking nothing until you see 'em yourself. Ronnie, oh Ronnie. This is so important. I need you to see this with me. I really need you with me now.'

Ronnie saw no humour in his face and softened immediately. 'Well, we can't leave the kids.'

'The kids, yeah the kids . . . kids!! kids!!'

While he prodded his family into their clothes and out of the house, Neary collected cameras, binoculars, opera glasses and blankets.

'Are we going to a drive-in?' Brad asked, still half-asleep.

'You stole my luminous paints,' Toby remembered.

'You'll get your luminous paint!' Neary was jubilant. 'Everything's going to be luminous!'

He got everyone as far as the kitchen, where Ronnie diverted to the refrigerator. She opened the door and grabbed her raw vegetable pouch. The refrigerator light was an unappetising green, and Toby said, 'That green light makes me barf.'

'I'll change it after I lose another three pounds,' his mother told him for the twentieth time.

74

Neary started hustling them all out of the house again and toward the family's Chevy station wagon parked around the back of the driveway.

'Roy,' Ronnie was leaking steam. 'You've proved your point. We all got out of the house. Now can we go back to bed?'

Instead of answering, Neary started shoving the children inside the car.

'This is only funny if it ends here in the driveway,' Ronnie said, going around to her side of the car.

'You promised Goofy Golf,' Toby said from the middle seat. His eyes were already closed again.

Finally, everyone was in. Ronnie had not closed her door and the ceiling light inside the car was still on. For the first time Ronnie saw it. Neary was red on one half of his face. Bright red.

'Roy, what is that? You're sunburned.'

Neary peered into the rear view mirror. This visible evidence made him even redder. 'Holy shit,' he whispered. 'I guess I took my vacation while you were sleeping.'

'But it's only half your face.'

But Neary was already backing down the driveway, returning to where the excitement had been most extreme.

He drove quickly to the place where it had all happened, pulled off the road and stopped near the scattered snow fence. The farmer and his family were gone, leaving behind some Colonel Sanders' boxes and one bottle of Wild Turkey.

Ronnie and the kids sounded like a sleeping symphony of troubles. But Roy was on point. He kicked circles for a while in the cool early morning, waiting . . . waiting for what? Waiting for the experience to come again. Please come again, he thought to himself. Why had something that was so frightening become so enthralling. He wanted seconds but now the dark was playing tricks.

The police weren't with him now. He was alone out here. Did they like people who waited alone? Was it easier to get away when . . . ?

Something woke Ronnie. She glanced back and saw her three children snoring against each other. And then there was her husband pacing back and forth nervously, eyes skyward. She got out, closing the car door softly, and fell into step.

'What are we doing here, Roy? Why won't you tell me what you're waiting for?'

'You'll know it when you see it,' he told her without confidence.

'Come on,' Ronnie said. 'I came here with you. I'm taking this very well. Now tell me. What did it look like?'

Roy waited, stared up and down the road, watched the sky a moment longer, then – 'Kind of . . . like an ice cream cone.'

This was almost too much for Ronnie. 'What flavour?' she asked with murderous innocence.

But Neary took her seriously. 'Orange. It was orange . . . and it wasn't really like an ice cream cone . . . it was sort of in a shell . . . this . . .' He made sculpting motions with both hands.

'Like a taco?'

'No, rounder, larger . . . and sometimes . . . it was like . . . like . . . you know, those rolls we had yesterday?'

'Bran muffins?'

'No! Not for breakfast!' Neary was conscious that his wife was humouring him and also running out of humour, but he persisted anyway. 'For dinner. What were those rolls? Those curvy ones?'

'You mean the crescent rolls?' she exclaimed, as though dealing with a Romper Room student.

'Yeah!' he said, excited all over again. 'And it gave off a kind of neon glow.'

That was definitely too much for Ronnie. She reached into her Baggie for a carrot. Neary walked a few paces away from her munching and hunched down near a rock, eyes heavenward again. Ronnie watched him anxiously. Obviously Roy was going through something ... something she couldn't begin to understand, but, apparently, it was important to him. Maybe she had been too bitchy.

Ronnie approached Roy and used her favourite Little Miss Marker voice. 'Don't you think I'm taking this really well?'

He didn't answer but stood up, still looking at the stars starting to fade in the ever lightening sky.

Ronnie looked up too and gave a little shudder. She didn't know why but she was slightly frightened. It was all a little weird. A lot weird.

'Snuggle,' she said to him.

Neary dutifully put his arm around her and drew her to him, Ronnie put her arms around his waist and began to nibble his ear.

'I remember when we used to come to places like this to look at each other.' She said it like Bambi.

Neary looked down at her and, seeming to remember some good old times, he smiled. Ronnie smiled back and gently sucked on Roy's upper lip.

He had always gone for that in a big way, and soon their kisses spread inside. But Roy was not so engrossed that he couldn't weasle open half an eye and turn it to the skies. Because that's precisely when everything exploded with a blue-hot fire-whoosh that tore at his clothes. Neary almost jumped out of his skin as the red lights diminished in the distance, but Ronnie knew it was only a semi-truck-trailer, and after a few seconds so, glumly, did Roy.

The spell was broken.

Ronnie, testing her husband, asked, 'If one of those things came down right now and the door opened, would you go on it?'

Roy, thrilled at the proposition, cried, 'Jesus Christ, yes!' Then, seeing and feeling the hurt tense through her, he added, 'Well, anyone would.'

But the damage was done. Ronnie broke away from him, and went back toward the car. He hurried after her.

Ronnie stopped and turned on him. 'You know what you've done to us?' she cried out. 'You know what this means? You've brought us out here twenty miles from home in the middle of the night ... and you have destroyed our sleep cycle. Your sons are gonna conk out in the middle of the day and Sylvia will be up until one a.m. for the next three nights because their father swears he saw a flat, orange Betty Crocker crescent roll that flies. We might as well all have breakfast right now.'

She paused to catch her breath and then in a lower tone, completed the demolition. 'Don't ever try anything like this again. We're your family. It is not normal.'

There was nothing that Ronnie could have said, Neary knew, that could have been more final. It sure wasn't normal, but as Neary was about to discover, normality as he once knew it was coming to an end.

ELEVEN

There is no fast way to get to Benares. The ancient and most holy city of the Hindus is approachable mainly through faith.

An approach by military aircraft was out of the question. To have sent a fighter plane or attack bomber through India's airspace would not only have freaked out the militantly neutral Indians but, more importantly, would have endangered the secrecy of the Project.

David Laughlin supposed, privately, that if there had been time, Lacombe would have travelled to Benares in the proper manner, on bare feet, wearing a loincloth and supported by a wooden staff. As it was, Laughlin was grateful for the small, fourteen-passenger Corvette jet borrowed from Air Alsace, which made the trip from Paris to Rangoon in just half a day.

A Vertol chopper brought them in low over the spires and domes of Benares a half hour later, as the sun was setting. The river moved sluggishly beneath the helicopter, its holy waters freighted with the holiest of silt.

The hillside lay a few miles outside the city. The Vertol hovered at a discreet distance while its pilot tried to find a place to land. It wasn't easy.

'Look at them!' Laughlin said. 'Thousands!'

'Tens of thousands,' Lacombe corrected.

'It's fantastic. I—'

'The Saddhu is a very holy man,' Lacombe cut in

quietly, above the rotor noise. 'But also very practical. He also wants an answer. In his lifetime. He has been listening for many years, With him it is more than a matter of faith. It is a matter of results.'

Laughlin thought that over. 'But I thought the Hindus went the other way,' he shouted. 'Nirvana, not here.'

Lacombe shrugged.

The chopper set down gently in a space near two Mercedes tour buses. The pilot cut the engines and the rotors whined down. Dust started settling over everything within a hundred yards. Lacombe climbed out first and stood momentarily in the brilliant sunset with Laughlin and two technicians.

The blood-red orange rays of the sun were coming in almost horizontally now. In a little while the great hot ball of flame, filtered and distorted by endless miles of dusty atmosphere, would swell, darken and hide itself from sight behind the low range of hills to the west.

'Let us go,' Lacombe said.

Laughlin gestured to the two technicians, who picked up their microphones, Magra tape recorder, portable battery-belts, and the lightweight Arriflex 16mm camera. The four men moved slowly through the crowd of pilgrims.

The people were densely packed, some on small rugs, with baskets of food beside them. There were whole families, even ancient grandparents who were probably under forty years of age, wizened and emaciated by hunger and disease.

The Westerners moved with prudent speed up

the hillside toward the cleared area where the Saddhu sat, legs crossed beneath him in the lotus position, eyes shut, palms pressed together, elbows out to the side like some strange, meditative bird of passage.

A sleek young Brahmin in city whites arose at Lacombe's approach. Laughlin moved in to translate while the technicians began setting up.

'It lacks half an hour of the sun's death,' the Brahmin told Lacombe.

His accent bothered Laughlin. Smooth, Oxonian English. The young man wore well-shined chukka boots, pipestem-thin trousers of white muslin, and a collarless jacket of the same fabric. He looked too urbanised for this place, his smooth flow of talk too glib. But even the holiest of men, Laughlin thought, needed managers.

The Saddhu himself moved not a muscle. By not even the flicker of an eyelid did he acknowledge anything around him of this world. Lacombe stood in contemplative silence for a moment, then lowered himself to a lotus seat near to, but at a respectful distance from, the Saddhu.

The microphones were ready now, each in its parabolic reflector. The Arriflex was to be hand held. Lacombe had insisted that it not be mounted on a tripod. He wanted the technician to keep it on his shoulder to have the mobility to photograph ... whatever there was to photograph.

His eyes closed, the Frenchman seemed to relax, although his back was stiffly erect. Out of the corner of his mouth, in French, he murmured an order to Laughlin, who turned to the audio technician.

'He wants to make sure you shield the Nagra.'

'Why?' the man wanted to know. 'We're nowhere near any electrical interference.'

'He's had bad luck before with tape recordings. The capstan motor usually conks out and the recording heads lose magnetism.'

'No kidding,' the technician said. 'Well, if he says so.' He produced a large, copper-mesh, boxlike affair, a shield that he placed over the small precision Nagra recorder. Then, shoving copper spikes into the earth, he grounded the shield carefully. 'Does that suit the mother?'

Laughlin wondered, and not for the first time, what they were doing in this strange place, with all these thousands, waiting . . . waiting for what? The report spoke of an event strictly unbelievable, but Lacombe had shown him how to suspend disbelief, to open himself to the incredible.

Laughlin turned away and watched the bloated disk of the sun as the hills to the west began biting a chunk out of its lower rim. In a moment only half the sun was visible. The Saddhu stirred slightly.

What happened next seemed to be in slow motion to Laughlin. He watched the Saddhu's outturned elbows pull in toward his emaciated brown ribcage. The palms of his hands, still pressed together, began a slow separation until only the fingertips still touched.

The Saddhu's eyelids slowly rose, like shutters on temple windows. His eyes, open, were enormous, jet black, ringed all the way around by white, the white then ringed by glossy black lashes.

The Saddhu's body stirred. Slowly, without apparent effort, he began to rise from the lotus to a standing position. The sleek city Brahmin sank to his knees. Laughlin found himself sitting down abruptly, as if the only person who had any right to be on his feet was the Saddhu. Out of the corner of his eye, Laughlin could see the audio technician and the camera fall, incredibly, to their knees. He was sure they had no idea what they were doing.

With grave deliberateness, the Saddhu's bare arms spread out from his body like the powerful wings of some great land-locked bird ready to take to the skies. Behind him, all that was left of the sun was the thinnest edge of rind. As Laughlin watched, the sun snuffed out. Darkness fell instantly.

The Saddhu's long arms swung up at his sides to shoulder height. They paused, then continued their upward sweep until the gnarled backs of his hands touched each other high over his head. They paused again. Then he brought the arms down in one great sweep – a conductor cueing a mighty orchestra.

From ten – twenty thousand throats came a low, melodious note. They sustained it with such power that it began to eat its way into Laughlin's brain. He noticed Lacombe's eyes snap open and swing sideways, cursing the technicians. Laughlin gestured. The audio man started the Nagra. Laughlin could see its reels turning through the copper mesh.

Now the Saddhu brought his arms up and cued another note, an interval above the first, higher on the scale. His worshippers filled the world with two tones, alternating them, sounding them separately and together – a minor interval, Laughlin thought, less than a third. A minor third? Not quite.

The Saddhu produced another note and then another and another. Now Laughlin began to lose a sense of the melody in the harsh cacophony of many voices. The ground beneath him seemed to vibrate with the intensity of the notes, unmelodic, strange to Western ears, notes the report had stated had come down from the stars four nights ago and that the Saddhu and his followers had been sounding each night since.

The intervals were never whole, Laughlin felt. They were quartered, halved, bent slightly into microtone steps. Each singer changed the notes slightly, making a raw, elemental howl. It soared skyward in a great chant, somehow ominous. It shook the earth beneath Laughlin but it also made the air itself vibrate.

The tropical twilight was now night. Damp blackness had descended upon them all. And, even though they could no longer see their Saddhu, the many thousands continued their chant, forcing it to grow to an almost unbearable intensity.

The stars had come out overhead. Laughlin gazed upward, shaking with the fierceness of the singing around him. He watched the star at the end of the Big Dipper's handle. It grew brighter, waned, brightened again. There was a frequency to it, like a message in Morse code. And then it . . . exploded.

A bright crimson flash illumined the upturned faces of the multitude. Lacombe was on his feet now, standing beside the Saddhu. The cameraman had swung his shoulder-braced Arriflex upward.

The crimson light elongated into a rolling pillar, turned orange. Then yellow. Then pale green. It hovered in the sky and suddenly the heavens were filled with the same five notes. The same chord, played on something that was not human. Pure.

Melodic. Clean. The worshippers below fell silent. And once again the sky sang down to them.

'Goddamn!' the cameraman said.

The pillar of fire winked out. The song ended.

The worshippers below sank back, faces pressed to the earth. The Saddhu turned to Lacombe.

'The sky,' he said in a thin voice, 'the sky sings to us.'

The two men embraced. Tears ran down the Frenchman's cheeks. His voice was thick with emotion.

'It sings to all of us, my friend.'

TWELVE

Several hours later that morning, Saturday, Neary stood bleary-eyed in front of the bathroom mirror, trying to organize enough of himself to at least get the shaver working. Brad, Toby, and a couple of the neighbours' kids were tearing around the house, shouting 'Goofy Golf' and other obscenities. Eventually, Roy took the can of Rapid Shave and nozzled a mound of white lather into the palm of his right hand. He automatically lifted the cream mountain toward his face when something mind boggling stopped him.

Neary began to stare at the stuff in his hand. He cocked his head and brought the lather mound eye level, then vaguely began to shape some of it with the middle finger of his left hand.

'No, that's not right,' Neary said to himself, not really conscious of what he was doing or saying. But this image was reminding him of something – something maddeningly out of mental reach – he knew this shape so well and yet it felt as if the connection was a million miles away. Neary blinked a little distressed. Everybody experiences something like this he thought – a moment, an image that seems so familiar, a person you've seen before but really never have, a place you think you visited once but knew you never did. These were flashes that some psychologists like to call *déjà vu*; and always pass in a matter of seconds. This flash was sure taking its time passing. It lingered for minutes, and so did Neary's eyes on that sloppy mound of Rapid Shave. Then . . .

The appearance of Ronnie – in the mirror – standing in the bathroom doorway brought Roy part way back.

'Ronnie,' he said. 'What does this remind you of?'

She totally ignored the lather mound, and said firmly, 'We're going to tell people at the party tonight that you fell asleep under a sunlamp on your right side.'

'What? What for?'

'I don't want to hear you talking about it at the party' she said. 'Not till you know what you're talking about.'

'If I don't talk about it,' he said, essaying logic, 'how am I gonna find out what's to know?'

'Talk about it with your buddies in the Department, not at parties.'

'What does the Department know?'

During this meeting of the minds, Brad and Toby had wandered into the bathroom.

'Dad, are they for real?' Brad asked.

'No, they're not for real,' Ronnie snapped.

'Don't tell him that,' Neary said.

'Mom . . . I believe in them,' Brad persisted.

'No, you don't.'

'Dad says so.'

'He does not,' Ronnie said. Then, pleadingly, 'Roy?'

'I just want to know what in the world is going on,' Neary admitted, the mound of foam still balanced in his right hand.

'It's just one of those things,' Ronnie said, matter-of-factly, as if that resolved everything.

'Which things?'

'I don't want to hear about this any more.'

'Do they live on the moon?' Toby asked.

'They got bases on the moon,' Brad said, really getting into it, 'so at night they can come in your window and pull the covers off!'

Ronnie shut her eyes. 'I'm not listening to this, I don't hear it.'

'Last night,' Neary said, as calmly as he could, 'I saw something I can't explain.'

Her fierce blue eyes snapped open and she fixed him in the mirror with her glare. 'Last night, at four a.m., I saw something I can't explain. A grown man –' Ronnie stopped abruptly, sensing the boys' full attention.

'Ronnie, you know I'm going out there again tonight, damn it!'

She turned to leave, and said lightly, 'No, you're not.'

'Yes,' he said, with a dramatic pause, 'I am.'

The phone began ringing.

Ronnie turned back, and said, playfully again, 'No, you're not.' She reached into the bathroom, grabbed his right wrist and planted his palm upward into his face. The shaving foam gooshed and Neary looked like a bathtub toy.

Roy stared at himself in the mirror. The white foam emphasised the reddish colour of his cheek. He smeared some of the foam onto his chin and other cheek. 'It ain't a moonburn, goddamn it,' he muttered to himself.

Neary had started shaving when Ronnie reappeared in the mirror. She looked like someone who had just been told something awful. Tears began to come out of her eyes and she just stood there in the doorway shaking.

Roy turned around immediately, saying, 'O.K., Ron . . . I don't have to go.'

'R-roy,' she said, 'that was Grimsby, from the Department.'

'Huh?'

'You're fired, Roy.' Ronnie was really sobbing now and she collapsed into his arms, cheek against his cheek, tears and lather. 'They . . . he wouldn't even talk to you. What are we going to do? You got fired? What's going on?'

'Jesus!' Neary said, stunned. He just stood there, razor in one hand, face smeared like a real bozo, his wife sobbing against him, looking at everything in the mirror and seeing none of it.

'Roy, what are we going to do?'

Neary, still stunned, didn't really hear her. His eyes, fixed in space, finally focused on a white object that he saw through the open bathroom door in the bedroom. It was a pillow on their bed. It had been left in a pushed-together, lumpy shape just like the shaving cream earlier.

'No,' Neary muttered to himself. 'That's not right.'

THIRTEEN

When you're a victim of instant unemployment, Neary thought, you should have plenty of time on your hands to mull things over. Things like orange cones that tan your skin and won't show up again to prove their existence to your wife.

He'd gone back the next night. Of course. And when none of the strange objects or colours appeared, he swore he was going to give up the whole idea. But the night after that he returned again.

The people he found there were getting to know each other. Old friends. The farmer in his pickup, with his pint bottle of whisky, was on hand. So was a lady who had brought along a rocker and sat there doing needlepoint, to fill in the time before the next appearance of what everybody had taken to calling 'the night things.' Another elderly woman had an album of photographs of 'them,' the by-product of other nights in other places. A sound made everyone look toward the northern skies. Jet aircraft could be heard passing in the rarified distance. 'We'll be here all night if that keeps up,' one of the elderly people complained. Roy knelt down by a lady who was eighty if she was a day. 'Are they coming over tonight?' he whispered gently. Those words were like magic, for her very pressed face blossomed years off her as though Neary had told her the meaning of life. She became teary-eyed, saying, 'Oh, I hope so. Don't you?'

'Yes, he answered her in all seriousness. The old lady measured his fervour, blinked an eye and hefted to her lap a leatherette volume-sized photo album. She opened it to the first page.

'I took these myself,' she said smartly. 'Out by the Parochial School.'

Neary looked at her six colour snapshots, a splash of yellow, a slit of white, a blur of out-of-focus blue. Anybody who didn't know how to use a camera produced mistakes like that for the first few rolls of film.

It wasn't that they were kooks, the kind of crazies who were always sighting flying saucers. It was just that except for her, Neary didn't sense in any of them the same yearning need he had to find out what had happened. They seemed content simply to witness it, like the crowd at the circus who watches the fire-eater spew great sheets of flame but doesn't care how he does it.

The second night after the 'night things' had appeared, quite a crowd seemed to have collected. There were people Neary couldn't remember seeing before. And, for the first time, he noticed the young woman and her little boy whom he'd pulled from the path of the wildly careening police cruisers.

Neary nodded to her over the heads of the crowd. She took her boy's hand and came over. 'You do remember us?'

'How can I forget?'

'Jillian Gu..er,' she said, shaking his hand. 'This is Barry.'

'Roy Neary. That was some night, wasn't it?'

'It doesn't feel like it's over.' She touched his cheek. 'You're sunburned.'

'Hoping to tan the other side tonight.'

'It got my face and neck.' She opened her blouse to reveal the upper curve of her breasts and the hollow at the base of her throat.

She watched as Roy's cheek turned a shade darker. 'I'm sorry,' she said, buttoning up. 'I just had the feeling you were my oldest friend.' She laughed. 'It only takes one experience like that, doesn't it?'

Neary nodded, no longer embarrassed. As he did so, a genial-looking man in unmatching slacks and a sports jacket shone a flashlight on them. Their sunburns seemed to stand out in his beam. This seemed to please him and with a Pentax and strobe, he snapped their picture. Jillian blinked and turned toward him as the man focused at little Barry, sitting near the fence and playing with a mound of dirt.

Moving swiftly, Jillian got in the way of the amateur photographer. 'He's a little young to have a record,' she told him angrily.

Neary watched the man cough up an apology and ankle away. 'Where do you think he's from?'

'Earth,' Jillian muttered bitterly. She bent down to wipe dirt off Barry's face. He was busily patting together a tall, conical mound.

'I, uh, have three of my own at home,' Neary announced.

'Did you tell your wife about what we saw?'

'Of course.'

'What does she think?' Jillian asked.

'She understands,' Neary said with some sarcasm 'perfectly.'

Jillian grinned. 'I called my mother to tell her.

She said that's what I got for living alone.' She paused and Neary saw that in some way she felt embarrassed, as he had before at the sight of her breasts – well, part of them.

'I'm not alone at all,' she covered quickly. 'There's Barry and the neighbours and I'm...not really...alone at all.'

'Barry's father?'

'Died.' She paused. She looked away from him. 'I don't suppose he'd have understood this any better than your wife does.'

There was nothing Neary could think of to say at this point. Instead he hunkered down to Barry's level and helped him pat dirt into place. 'Working kind of late tonight, huh, kiddo?'

'I know he should be in bed,' Jillian said in a guilty tone. 'But after the way he ran off the other night, I'm not letting him out of my sight.'

Neary nodded. He stared for a moment at the cone of dirt the little boy had built. He fingered a twig and etched fluted sides into the mound. 'Hm.' He reached for some pebbles nearby. 'Try these,' he offered.

Barry arranged them around the base of the cone, as if they were boulders thrown there by some explosion of natural forces. 'That's better,' Neary said. Oddly enough both the boy and his mother accepted this as perfectly natural behaviour.

'Hey!' Neary asked, suddenly puzzled. 'What does this remind you of?'

Jillian dug deep for an answer but she didn't know what. Then she bent over Barry to gently rough up the smooth side facing her. 'I like it better like so,' she said.

'Me, too,' he breathed.

'Here they come!' a voice shouted.

'Out of the Northwest!' someone yelled.

Neary and Jillian looked in the direction everyone was pointing. A hush descended over all. Adults and juveniles raised binoculars and cameras. On somebody's transistor radio the Eagles were singing 'Desperado'.

'There!' Jillian said pointing.

Two foggy pinpoints of light shifted back and forth, rising, falling, growing brighter in the darkness.

Neary raised his camera. 'I'm ready this time.'

She had placed her hand on his arm. 'You're trembling.'

'I know.' Neary laughed recklessly. 'What if we're just two whackos standing on a hill with a dozen other loonies?'

'Your eyes burn, don't they?'

'For two days now.'

'Mine, too.'

'But this is crazy,' he said, his teeth almost chattering. 'It's like Hallowe'en for grown-ups.'

The lights were bearing down on them inexorably now, blinding, larger, merciless, painful to watch. 'Trick or treat?' Jillian asked then.

Neary aimed his camera, but he had begun shaking so badly he wondered what kind of picture he'd get. 'If those things stop and open their doors,' he asked her, 'would you get in and go?'

'If those things stop, I'm going home.'

'Listen,' Neary said. 'The sound . . . listen.'

The gathering in the field stirred as an unusual

sound came over them, permeating the air. It was a rhythmical noise, blowing against the wind – louder now. And suddenly it was coming faster and more frenzied than any of them had expected. and fear shot through them all as they tried and failed to interpret the internal combustive pounding and ... two blinding anti-collision lights swallowed their world. The very air was displaced. And with the sky like summer noon, the lights suddenly gave way, clearly revealing two Air Force Huey helicopters that descended howling upon pockets of the idle curious, beating on them with hot air, gas exhaust, sucking dirt, napkins and human debris up into the spiraling convections, and still the screaming machines manoeuvred around each other until even aluminium chairs, card tables, blankets and picnic leavings were sent up and distributed to the next county. 'This is crazy,' he said.

In dismay, in self-disgust and in some anger, too, he watched the two Air Force helicopters hover a dozen feet above them.

Neary saw the little old woman with the snapshots as he chased after them, whirling wildly in the wash from the two choppers, whose beams blinded her.

Barry screamed. He jumped and began to run. Jillian grabbed him. 'Barry, it's only helicopters, Barry.'

'Yeah,' Neary shouted over the noise and dust. 'They're ours.'

The downwash from the rotors had set a roadsign trembling. Neary watched it vibrate for a moment, just as the road sign had vibrated that other night. Then it had seemed wild, supernatural, something caused by ... well, perhaps by night things.

Now he could see quite plainly that a sign was vibrating in the harsh wind of a manoeuvring helicopter. It was happening right here in front of a hundred witnesses.

And for the first time in this whole insane affair, Neary began to doubt not only what he'd seen, but what he'd thought about it.

FOURTEEN

Out here in the desert the stars were big and hard as diamonds. Some of the stars closest to the horizon scintillated from all the rising heat released after another desert scorcher.

It was midnight in Barstow, California, and the monstrous parabolic ear of the Goldstone Radiotelescope was listening to the sky. Station 14 was down for overhaul. That was the cover-story. But the same 210 foot dish that tracked the Viking, Helios, Pioneer, Mariner, Jupiter, Saturn and Voyager missions was honed in a state vector in 'deep space.' Inside the blockhouse a sign barked to all who entered: *Network Data Processing Activities. On-duty operation personnel only! Contact MC COPSCON 5883.* A handprint Ident. box blocked a vacuum-sealed doorway like a sentry. There was a lot of anxiety on this special night. A lot of angst . . . Six right hands pressed down on the sentry box, handprint identifications were made, and the door hissed open. It looked more like a storage area, than the mission control computing centre. The core of activity was a glass-enfolded cubicle that rested on a flatbed trailer in the centre of this otherwise dark and empty warehouse. Inside, the cubicle looked like a college fraternity prank. Two dozen project members were scrunched up to their shoulders in CRT's, telementry tracking hardware, command function consoles, transmitter and receiving units, and, most incongruous of all, a mini-Yamaha synthesizer and Claude Lacombe doing a five-note exercise on its keyboard. It seemed like he was sending a message. His fingers touched staccato, but the sound was undeniably India. Benares. The sky music. It was finally serving its hypothetical purpose.

And then came the response. The CRT readout was flooded with it. The hardcopy poured out of an IBM in reams. The paperwork was all over the floor, and project members were all thumbs trying to read it. It wasn't music coming back. It was numbers. For fifteen minutes there occurred a rush of pulses that dotted the paper. There were pauses and long intervals and then more rapid-fire communications. Lacombe was certain of that. Communication was taking place. He sat down and pressed his forehead to the palms of his hands. He took a breath and expelled the air, shuddering. The teletype noise was deafening to some of the younger people in this claustrophobic space, but when the chattering stopped it was Lacombe's heart that sank. Only when the communication resumed would the Frenchman settle back and almost smile.

'Okay, gang!' It was the Operations Advisor who was speaking now. 'Here's the pattern. We've received two fifteen minute broadcasts. 104 rapid pulses before a five-second pause, then forty-four pulses and another five seconds' rest, then thirty R.P.'s and a sixty-second interval before an entirely different set of signals, which go as follows: forty plus five. Thirty-six plus five. Ten, then sixty, rest, and back to 104.'

Lacombe played the five notes into the transmitting equipment and a Cal Tech advisor was quick to ask, 'What about a response to that?' Lacombe looked up at him and shrugged. Maybe tomorrow they would learn what the notes meant. But now, the race was on, and twenty-four Mission Advisors became think-tank executives.

One long haired man who slightly resembled Rod Stewart spoke first as he sorted through the repeated numbers. 'It's not my social security number. Too many digits.'

Somebody else quipped, 'Maybe it's how many Quarter Pounders Ronald MacDonald sold last month.'

A Texas boy spoke up next. He whistled and smiled in thought. 'That second set of numbers. 40–36–10 . . . could be a zoftig person with no hips.'

Everybody laughed at this except Lacombe. He didn't understand the joke and looked to his interpreter for the translation. But Laughlin didn't respond. He wasn't even looking at his employer, but instead was up to his armpits in hardcopy. Lacombe studied him. Laughlin was in a sweat over something, and when he looked up everyone but Lacombe was looking the other way. The Frenchman nodded to his interpreter, encouraging him to say what was on his mind. Laughlin did just that.

'Excuse me!'

Everyone was pondering the big question and talking amongst themselves, so Laughlin screwed on his lumberjack voice and overdid it slightly. 'EXCUSE ME!'

The room fell silent. Even the readouts stopped printing. Ironically, it was the end of a receiving cycle.

'Uh . . . before I got paid to speak French, I got

paid to read maps and that number looks a longitude to me.'

Nobody budged. Laughlin's opinion drew blank stares. So he went on. 'Two sets of three numbers, right? Well, the first number's got three digits, the last two are below sixty.'

Laughlin stood up and moved to join Lacombe. Lacombe was already on his feet ready to burst loose with Eurekas! The room remained in a stupefied silence. Then, as everyone grappled with the idea, a core of excitement formed in the centre of the group and rippled outward.

'Maybe...' someone spoke out, 'Maybe they're telling us a location in right ascencion and declination on the sky. Maybe giving us galactic coordinates.'

'No way, man,' someone was quick to say. 'That doesn't correspond to the direction of our "Big Ear". I think the man's right! I think we're getting terrestrial coordinates.' And that was the pin buster.

Every project official was screaming for a map. A burst of manpower left the audio cubicle and raced to the corridor, heading for the mission supervisor's office.

Inside the office a large globe rested in its steel cradle. Suddenly the door flew open and the hallway light spilled in. Dawn broke in Rand McNally's western hemisphere and excited project members rushed in like teenagers vandalising the principal's office. They tried to move the globe in its stand, but it must have weighed three hundred pounds. A mathematics wizard used his shoulders to pop the globe from its moorings and bobble it back into the corridor.

Other members formed a relay team and planet

Earth, tossed like a volleyball, rounded a corner and flew toward the communications cubicle. Once inside, Laughlin slapped away the extra fingers and traced the longitude from the south pole.

'Antarctica, ocean . . . ocean . . . ocean . . . just missing Easter Island, just missing Sala-Y-Gomex Island. Landfall in Mexico. Just missing Puerto Vallarta . . . crossing into New Mexico and picking up Carlsbad Caverns but continuing on and . . .'

Another man's fingers started tracing another line westward across the heartland of the United States. 'Maine . . . New Hampshire . . . Great Lakes . . . Minnesota . . . South Dakota . . .'

And then their fingers came together in the northeast corner of the state of—

'Wyoming?' Laughlin looked up at Lacombe. 'Wyoming.' The silence was shattered by the Texas drawl of the team leader.

'Well, don't just stand there like a bunch of penguins, get me a geodetic sectional map of Wyoming. Get me everything on it!'

Meanwhile Lacombe sat back down, donned his headphones, played the five musical tones into the great transmitter and waited, listening. Nothing. He keyed the Yamaha again. Nothing. Lacombe sat forward, intently. He played again, but this time the sounds were all but drowned out by two dozen project members celebrating their first definitive breakthrough.

FIFTEEN

The toy xylophone was poorly tuned. That was why the five notes sounded so strange when little Barry played them.

He didn't learn them all at once, Jillian noted from the other room. He had kept working on the tune until he got it . . . well . . . the way he wanted it.

To Jillian's ear, even though the tune was strange, Barry's chuckles were reassuring. He was there. He was happy. The tune's curious sequence of five notes – where do kids get these ideas? – was oddly disturbing, but of course these toy xylophones were never accurate. It was easy to make them sound . . . well . . . peculiar.

Jillian had spent the day, as she had the day before, making endless charcoal and pastel sketches. She had abandoned a career in art by the simple act of moving this far from big cities. But the habit of it was difficult to shake. She would find herself sketching Barry, a chair, a random arrangement on the kitchen table of a ketchup bottle, salt shaker and dirty plate.

Today she had been drawing landscapes, mountainous ones. In the way they looked – distant uneven rows of teeth, peaks at odd intervals – they somehow reminded her of the tune Barry kept repeating on his xylophone.

The purest form of total random choice made mountains look as they did, the merest chance criss cross of volcanic thrust and gravity and the beating down of weather over centuries of time.

Only random choice could have brought Barry to pick out those five notes, and yet once he chose them, he remained with them as if ... well, certainly, a randomness existed. It was all around them, in the way the veins in a leaf lay, unique to that leaf, never repeated in another. Each pebble on the beach was a bit different in size or contour or colour or texture from every other pebble.

But the way Barry sounded those notes it was almost as if in randomness there could be a message.

Jillian threw most of her sketches away in the cleanup process, but she saved one because it reminded her of something. She didn't remember what exactly. This particular mountain she had drawn was terribly tall and thin, needly and distorted like one of those desert spires formed when wind and sand have eaten away the softer stone to lay bare the core spout of harder lava that formed the ancient throat of a volcano.

Its sides were gashed by harsh grooves as it rose out of a desolate landscape like a misshapen finger thrust accusingly into the eye of the sun.

Thunder rumbled nearby. Jillian shivered and ran outside to see if rain was coming. Clouds had begun gathering in the west, obscuring the weak sun with masses of leaden gray. Behind the clouds Jillian could see lightning at work. A major electrical storm was coming. But the flashes were strangely prolonged, as if frozen. Small distant points of light began skipping from cloud to cloud.

The air began to thicken with the sound of

swarming bees. The clouds now seemed to be actually moving . . . down.

Yes, down and in toward her. Within them, strange flashes of coloured light seemed to ricochet from one cloud to another.

'No,' Jillian said in an undertone.

Across the rolling landscape, a kind of darker mass of cloud seemed to reach from the ground to the sky, a column that grew wider as it rose, almost like a . . . a tornado. Jillian felt defenceless, the way the girl Dorothy had felt in 'The Wizard of Oz' as a giant tornado loomed on the Kansas horizon.

But this isn't Kansas, Jillian told herself. And those bright coloured things dropping from cloud to cloud are not . . . not real? But of course they were real.

'No!' she shouted, suddenly frightened. Jillian eyed the safety of her house and turned slowly, very slowly taking the first of the long fifteen steps to the back door. She was terrified now and didn't want to make herself panic by running. She continued toward the house in a kind of crazed slow motion. Jillian entered the house and slowly and deliberately she shut the back door and locked it. She moved into the living room now and began lowering the blinds. As Jillian moved from room to room her movements unwillingly became faster. She went from a walk to a trot to a run, jerking the blinds down as panic took control of her hands and made her fumble and miss.

She stood still for a moment, trying to make sense of everything. That *had* been thunder, hadn't it? And lightning? That distant buzz, as of a swarm of bees, that had been something to do with the storm. And the clouds coming down toward her. But she'd never seen clouds do that before.

Barry was laughing. He'd never feared the violence of storms, for which Jillian decided she was probably grateful. But to hear the wholehearted way he laughed now as the thunder clashed and the lightning flared was a little too much for Jillian's peace of mind. No child had a right to be that happy.

She hurried into his room. He had stopped playing the xylophone and was standing at the only window in the house whose blind was still up. He was staring intently out at the sky and what he saw filled him with great glee.

He began running through the house, raising the blinds, swinging open doors and windows. 'Barry, no!'

Jillian ran after him, shutting, closing, locking. They came upon each other in the living room. The boy had just sent the shade rattling up.

Jillian pushed the boy to one side and yanked the blind shut. As if on cue, an immense roar of thunder shook the house. Behind the blind a flash of lightning flared with such an orange intensity that it seemed to set the entire wall aflame. The buzzing roared around her.

Jillian cringed from it, but Barry clapped his hands and laughed. Now the house was dark. Only the booming flashes of firelight outside illuminated it from moment to moment. Jillian took Barry's hand and led him to her bedroom, where she picked up the telephone book and began searching for Roy Neary's number.

As she did, another clap of thunder and orange

light bashed at the house like a giant fist. The television set went on. So did the stereo. Electric lamps began to switch off and on. She could hear, in the vastness of her storage closet, the distant sound of her vacuum cleaner starting up.

Barry broke away from her grasp, ran to the window and sent the blind skyward with one happy swoop. As he did, a strange stillness fell on the place. The television and stereo were quiet. The vacuum cleaner stopped. There was no sound at all, not even of wind or the distant buzz of insects.

Then Jillian heard it. It sounded like . . . claws.

On the roof. Scrambling across the shingles. Claws. Or talons. Long fingernails or toenails. Sharp, scurrying sounds.

She stared at the ceiling above her, eyes moving along in the direction of the scraping, scrambling noises. They stopped for a moment at the chimney.

And now they began to come down the chimney.

Jillian dashed into the living room and raced for the damper handle. At any cost, she had to shut the flue. Barry followed happily.

'Come in!' he shouted. 'Come in!'

The claw-like sounds skittered down the inside of the chimney. Jillian dived at the damper, slammed it shut.

Instantly, a harsh roar of noise shook the house. Orange light flooded every corner of the room. All the window shades snapped up.

Jillian dropped to the floor, hands over her ears. The television was blaring away. On the stereo, the turntable was revolving. From the loudspeakers, Johnny Mathis was singing 'Chances Are' in a huge voice like the growl of a lion.

111

Jillian ran for the telephone again, dragging Barry with her.

Eyes wide with fright now, she found Neary's number. As she held the telephone to her ear, instead of a dial tone, it gave forth the same five-note melody that Barry had been playing on his xylophone. Jillian jiggled the hook, got a tone like the angry *zzz* of bees, and dialled Neary's number. The room lights were doing strange things, dimming to a fitful smoky red, then flaring to a blue-white that hurt her eyes. The telephone was buzzing.

'Hello?' a woman asked.

'Roy?' Jillian's voice was a frightened croak.

'He's not here,' Ronnie said matter-of-factly. 'I'm his wife. Who's calling, please?'

The overload was so ferocious that even the air in the rooms seemed to burn orange-hot with a fearful buzzing noise. It was as if some giant high-tension tower, carrying thousands of volts, had toppled down on this house and charged it so thickly with power that—

The vacuum cleaner, like a prisoner being tortured in a cell, screamed in horror. The stereo speakers vibrated and burst apart.

A metal ashtray rose into the air and hovered for an instant, suspended in the terrifying heat of the air. She could hear the clattering on the roof again.

Jillian lost track of what was happening. The phone dropped from her hand. She slid to the floor. Barry was nowh—

'Barry!'

Racing into the room like an auto run amok, the vacuum cleaner began howling across the floor, chasing her as she jumped out of its way. It wheeled, charged again. Jillian ran.

In the horror of crashing, grinding noises and flashing, blinding lights, Jillian lost track of what was happening. Barry was . . .

'Barry!'

Somewhere in the distance she could hear over everything Barry's gleeful laughter. The kitchen. Jill, beyond walking, started the endless crawl across the room to the kitchen.

The refrigerator was vibrating intensely. The door swung open, the light inside blinking on and off spastically.

The she caught sight of her son. He, too, was crawling on the floor. Toward the dog door opening. He reached it and started trying to wriggle through the narrow opening.

Jillian lunged forward and grabbed for Barry's foot. She caught it and started to haul him back in. She pulled hard. He slid across the linoleum toward her. The air smelled brassy and dank with electricity.

Then something pulled him away. Some force was tugging him outside the house.

'Let go of him!' she screamed.

Jillian gritted her teeth and pulled back. The boy's body shifted forward and back a few inches.

Jillian held on to her son until she felt, she knew, that if she did not let go, he would be dislocated. Sobbing, Jillian loosened her grip and Barry slipped away from her hands and out the little door.

In a flash, he was gone.

Jillian heaved herself up off the floor and threw open the kitchen door, staggering into the back yard, but Barry was nowhere in sight. She saw the tornado-like formation hovering above the house, as if parked, lit up by the tiny geodesic points of flashing and busting lights.

Then the cloud eased away into the gathering darkness. And Jillian, not really knowing what she was doing, not really caring about anything any more, started to follow, started to chase after it, until an immense shape loomed up, gigantic arms enfolding her. All the breath came out of Jill. She fell to the stubble of a corn field.

Cringing, she glanced at the giant figure entangling her. A straw-stuffed scarecrow looked down, smiling his idiot grin, arms flapping loosely as she slapped them away. Jill had lost.

Barry was gone.

For a moment, Jillian lay there, sobbing in anger and pain. As she looked up through tears, she saw a lone star overhead change from white to blue to red.

And then disappear.

SIXTEEN

'What were you doing up on the garage roof?'
Ronnie asked.

Neary had come in and gone straight to the bathroom to wash. 'Some carpentry,' he shouted past
the noise of running water.

Ronnie went to the kitchen window and saw that
he had knocked together some sort of platform at
the peak of the garage, a platform on which a folding deck chair sat. 'It's a lookout, isn't it?' she
called.

She turned away from the window to find him
with his face buried in a towel, scrubbing himself
dry. 'Roy, instead of building platforms . . .'

She let the idea drop. She didn't want to become
the wife who nagged her unemployed husband into
finding work. But she also didn't want to be the
wife of the neighbourhood fruitcake, sitting up
there in his makeshift planetarium watching for
orange Betty Crocker cresc   rolls.

'You had a 'phone call,' she said.

He dropped the towel. 'Big storm toward Harper
Valley!' he announced. 'You can see for miles up
here!'

'She didn't give her name.'

'She?'

'Or wouldn't.' Ronnie took a small, measured
breath. 'Seemed kind of shattered to be talking to
your wife.'

'Who?'

'Hung up, finally, after a lot of thrashing-around noise.'

Neary nodded absentmindedly, his glance going past Ronnie to the kitchen clock. 'We don't have that much time. It's an hour's drive. Baby-sitter here yet?'

'She's here.' Ronnie took another small, cautious breath. 'Roy, I hope you understand that, after this, we can't be laying out money for baby-sitters. Not until . . .'

He had the good grace to look guilty. 'I know. I appreciate your going along with this, Ronnie.'

'But it's on one condition.'

'Which is?'

'That when the meeting is over, you drop the whole thing. Isn't that why the Air Force announced this meeting?'

The fifty-mile drive went slowly, Neary realized, because Ronnie was not in a talkative mood. They approached the outskirts of DAX Air Base with about ten minutes to spare before the start of the meeting, whose time had been announced over radio and TV for several days now.

Up ahead the first sentry post loomed. Ronnie sank down in her seat. 'I'll never forgive you,' she said, 'if we run into anybody we know here.'

He stopped to ask the sentry for directions to the Civilian Information Centre. 'It's that big all-glass building,' the corporal said, tucking a green visitor's pass in behind the windshield wiper. 'You can't miss it.'

'I sure can't,' Neary commented. The building was huge, flat and thin, like a matchbook on end, acres of picture windows framed in anodized aluminium mullions. He parked next to someone's battered old farm pickup truck, another green card on its windshield.

The waiting room of this all-glass skyscraper was huge, endless. A civilian woman sat at a desk, took Neary's name, and gave him a name-tag to wear, as she had the more than thirty people already sitting there.

'These people,' Ronnie whispered in Neary's ear as they sat down. 'They're all misled.'

'Shssh.'

'I knew it would be like this.'

'You don't know what you're talking about,' Neary whispered fiercely.

'Look at that one over by the elevators,' Ronnie whispered back. She indicated a woman in her late fifties, raddled, white hair flying in several directions at once, her gaze as empty as an ancient headstone.

'Halfway over the edge,' Ronnie murmured.

'On her way to the rocks below.'

Just then, Jillian Guiler came through the door, and the reporters came to life, surrounding her instantly.

'Could you give us a statement, Mrs. Guiler?' a reporter asked, as the hot lights were turned on her and the cameras started grinding.

Jillian, looking distraught and very tired, said nothing.

'Your report to the Police was ... ah ... really quite breathtaking. We'd like to make the six o'clock. We lose our young audience at eleven.'

Jillian seemed not to have heard.

Another journalist said to a colleague, 'That's her, isn't it? That's the lady in the clouds.'

Jillian stirred into life. 'Can *you* tell *me* what happened?' she demanded.

'Well, no, ma'm.'

'Then we have nothing to talk about.'

'But we understand no ransom note has been found.'

The first reporter tried to follow up. 'What about the F.B.I. story? Is there any truth to that . . . that the child is missing? You gave the police a report. Would you mind repeating it for television?'

Jillian started to panic. The questions were furious, maligning and irrational. Jill was retreating to the elevators when she caught Neary's eye across the room. As the elevator arrived she formed the words, 'They got him!'

'What?' Roy hadn't read her, but Ronnie sure did and buried her husband with one of her prize winning rotten looks as the elevator doors opened and swallowed Jillian from view.

A Master Sergeant in full-dress uniform came into the room.

'Folks . . . you can go in now. Room 3655. Just follow me.'

The Tolono Group, lead by Neary and Ronnie, headed for the corridor. TV news cameras were waiting this time just on the other side of the doors. On went the quartz lights and the cameras started to whir.

Ronnie jerked her purse up to cover her face, just as if she had been arrested. 'Damn you, Roy!' she muttered behind the bag.

The thirty or so civilian witnesses looked suddenly seedy, bleached out by the brilliant flood light from quartz bulbs in reflectors towering toward the ceiling of the room.

With the entrance of the Air Force team, and a phalanx of accompanying newspaper reporters and photographers, it became clear to Neary that whatever he had hoped to get from this meeting, what the Air Force wanted was publicity. So be it. For a change he and the military saw eye to eye. Let the whole world know what happened.

His initial feeling of satisfaction was dampened a bit when he saw that the Air Force spokesmen, all in civilian suits, would be sitting at ease on bent-plywood-and-foam-rubber contour swivel chairs, elevated on a platform a little above the rest of the room. In a hollow square around them ranged the voluntary witnesses, uncomfortable on folding chairs, unprepared for being the focus of so much publicity, still dressed for the most part in clothes they'd worn all day at work or on the farm.

'I'm Major Benchley,' the younger man mused. 'And this,' he continued, holding up a large colour blow-up of an eerie high resolution disc in blurred motion, 'is a flying saucer.'

That got everybody's attention, producing some 'oohs' and 'aahs,' and ad-libbed responses to the effect that 'I saw that one' and 'That's the one.'

'Made of pewter,' Benchley went on after the stir had subsided. 'Made in Japan. And thrown across the lawn by one of my children. I wanted to open up with this to show you that we're not all polished brass about these things and to make another point clear. Last year Americans took more than seven billion photographs, spending a record six-point-six-million on film equipment and processing. With all those clicking shutters, where is the indisputable photographic evidence that extraordinary phenomena exist in the skies over your homes?'

The 'witnesses' seemed stunned or intimidated in silence until one of the journalists said, 'How many times can we reach for our cameras when a sudden surprise catches us off-guard? How many actual automobile or plane crashes are filmed and make the evening news?'

There were sounds of general agreement from the Tolono Group, and one of the more rational of their number stood up and said, 'To dismiss out of hand the evidence for UFOs will not quiet the fears that we may be living through the first stages of exploration from elsewhere.'

'I am a reasonable person,' said the little old lady with the remains of her photo album. 'A reasonable person,' she repeated reasonably enough. 'All I know is that I saw something that was unlike anything I have ever seen before.'

Nobody spoke for a while so Neary raised his hand.

'Let someone else speak,' Ronnie hissed, reaching out to pull down his arm.

But Roy was already on his feet. 'Look, sir. You people run the sky, right? Have you looked in the sky recently? There's a circus going on up there.'

'I can only reiterate,' the major said, 'that after ten years with the Air Tactical Intelligence and the Office of Special Investigations there has been no indisputable proof of the physical existence of these things.'

'Which things?' Neary asked.

Major Benchley had leaned over to confer with two colleagues. Now he straightened up and peered at Roy's name tag. 'Please understand me, Mr. Neary. I'm not attacking your credibility...'

'That's O.K. Just tell us what's going on.'

'We're not sure. We can't just assume, as you seem to, that these were excursion vehicles from another planet.'

'Well, it sure wasn't the Goodyear blimp,' Neary said.

Many of the 'witnesses' laughed. Ronnie did not.

'Let's say it's foreign technology,' the Major said in a conciliatory tone. 'Why assume it's *that* foreign.' He gestured with his thumb to the sky.

'Fine. Great,' Neary responded. 'Let's say the Russians are building and flying them. So what are they doing in Indiana airspace?'

That got a laugh from everyone – Air Force, civilians, press and 'witnesses'.

Major Benchley waited for order and started over. 'We have had some high-altitude refuelling missions in the visible vicinity, and I'm told of a high build-up of static electricity – heat lightning. Also we have a condition called temperature inversion whereby a layer of cold air is sandwiched between layers of warm air.'

Neary looked around the packed conference with mock incredulity. 'You guys called this meeting to tell us what's going on and all we're getting are weather reports.'

'What would you like to believe is going on?'

Ronnie tried to pull Roy down, but he took her hand away and said, 'I'd like to believe the United States Air Force knows.' Then he sat down.

'Who's going to pay for the damage to my land?'

Major Benchley blinked. 'Pardon me?'

'I own the land where these people have been squatting at night,' said the man, whom Roy recognised as the well-to-do gentleman he had noticed earlier. 'This man over here,' – he indicated Neary – 'tore down several yards of my snow fence. There's trash all over the place from where these people have been staying up all night, eating Kentucky Fried Chicken and drinking beer. Who's going to pay for it all?'

Major Benchley pointed a finger at the landowner. 'Did you see anything that night?'

The man laughed. 'My family has owned that piece for more than eighty years and we've never seen one damn thing.'

The television cameras had swung quickly to the landowner, and Neary realized that the meeting was starting to fall apart. If he didn't jump in fast, the focus would be lost forever.

'Wait a goddamn minute!' he said loudly, sensing Ronnie physically edge away from him as he jumped to his feet again. 'I saw something.' The cameras swiveled back to him. 'This thing has cost me my job! That's how serious it is to me. It happened to me, it happened to some of you, and we want to know what it is!'

Benchley had begun talking over the last of his words. 'If the evidence is good the case will stand up and the existence of extraordinary phenomenon will have to be taken seriously.'

'We are the evidence!' Roy shouted. 'And we want to be taken seriously.'

'Please, Mr. Neary.'

'Please, Major Benchley,' Neary mimicked him. 'I would like to believe that I'm not going crazy. There are other people in this room who saw what I saw and they would like to believe that they are not going crazy. Is that not a reasonable request?'

Major Benchley was silent for several moments and when he spoke again it was spontaneous. 'I think there are all sorts of things that would be great fun to believe in. Time Travel and Santa Claus for instance. You know, everybody, I wish I'd seen it. For years I've wanted to see one of those darn silly things hopping around in the sky, because I believe in life in the universe. But ... odds are against there not being life. The extraterrestrial hypothesis is merely one of many alternate possibles. We seem to want proof that out there is something that can solve our problems for us. It's an emotional situation we have here. We want answers too, not mysteries.'

Neary sunk into his aluminium folded chair.

'Can you tell us – is your Air Force base conducting any tests in the Tolono area? You know – secret testing maybe?'

Major Benchley hesitated again and then, looking straight at Neary, said, 'It sure would be easy to lie to you and say yes. You'd walk away with an answer you could live with. But this is not the case and I won't mislead you. To tell you the truth, I don't know what you saw.'

Neary smiled, and then said, 'You can't fool us by agreeing with us.'

That produced a burst of laughter, which confused Neary for a moment. He had meant what he said; it was not a joke.

Benchley laughed, too. Then he held up his hand for quiet, saying, 'You must understand, all of you, that there are other considerations at work here. A certain hysteria sets in. We've had some schoolchildren burned quite seriously because they were playing with flares. Tonight we even heard from a lady in Harper Valley who blames this thing for the disappearance of her four-year-old son.'

It was at this point that the old farmer decided to share his experience with everyone. 'I saw Big Foot once,' he announced. 'It was up in the Sequoia National Park. The winter of Nineteen Fifty-One. It had a foot on him, thirty-seven inches, heel to toe. Made a sound I would not want to hear twice in my life.'

'What about the little star of Bethlehem that led the three wise men to Jesus?' an addled lady with bluish hair and a Gideon bible asked. 'This star has never been satisfactorily explained by astronomers.'

The television cameramen were having a wonderful time.

'Sir, is there any truth at all to this Loch Ness monster crap?'

As they were heading through the lobby for the outside, Major Benchley came up to them, his right hand outstretched.

'Mr. Neary,' he began. 'I just want to say—'

'Why the hell did your helicopters blow up off that ridge without any warning the other night?' Roy shouted. 'What the hell is that?'

'Roy?'

'Mr. Neary, I don't know what you're talking about. I just came over to—'

'I don't believe you!' Neary exploded. 'I don't believe anything you say, Benchley.'

Benchley, truly stunned by this outburst, backed off.

Ronnie pulled Neary away from the officer with both hands. 'Roy,' she said. 'Stop it! Stop it!' She pushed him across the lobby in the general direction of a Coke machine, and went back to make their apologies to the major.

Neary fed his coins into the machine and, Coke in hand, wandered off down a corridor, trying to cool off, trying to figure out what was the matter with him. He wasn't like that, blowing off at guys unprovoked. Benchley hadn't really done anything to him; the guy was just doing his job.

Roy caught himself staring at a small opening along one long wall. Still sipping away at his Coke, he swung open the panel door and there was a master control circuit box, an array of hundreds of circuit-breaker switches.

Neary's forefinger traced the office diagram for the building that was tacked to the inside of the panel door. Then, moving quickly, he began snapping circuit breakers off here and there. His fingers flipped back and forth as he checked the diagram, threw another set of switches, consulted the diagram and flipped off more circuits.

'Roy!' Ronnie had found him.

Neary was smiling now. Shutting the panel door, he took Ronnie's arm and escorted her out of the building to the parking lot.

'Roy, what's the matter with you?'

'I'm fine. Everything's fine, just fine.' He felt foolishly pleased with himself.

Neary started the engine and gunned the car out of the lot toward the sentry post. A line of cars were stopped there, drivers and passengers – civilian and military – standing by their cars, looking back toward the tall glass building. He braked to a stop at the end of the line, and he and Ronnie got out, too.

It had come out just right. He'd darkened some offices and turned the lights on in others. Across the entire broad face of the DAX Air Force Administration Facility, shining forth into the night for people to see for miles around, the windows spelled out three letters: UFO.

The photographer and reporter looked at the week's worth of unwrapped newspapers strewn across the lawn, the bottles of spoiling milk in the delivery box, and then at each other. They continued up the walk to Jillian Guilder's house and rang the door bell.

They rang the bell for several minutes and knocked on the door several more. They tried peering through the drawn blinds and then went around to the back door and tried that. But they were unsuccessful. They were convinced that Jillian was somewhere inside the dark house. Their FBI and police sources had assured their editor that she was. But, eventually they gave up and went away.

Inside, Jillian had boarded up every window. The living room in chaos, as were the kitchen and her bedroom. Although she'd cleaned up the mess in

the kitchen, the rest of the rooms were beyond her
– even making the bed had become impossible –
and the house remained much as it had been since
the night Barry had been taken and the day after,
when the police and the FBI men went through it
and the fields and woods surrounding the house,
searching for clues.

She had taken all the phones in the house off
their hooks. The police and the FBI had nothing to
tell her; they'd had nothing to tell for the week that
Barry had been gone. They said that if he'd been
kidnapped, the kidnappers would have been in
touch days ago. They didn't tell her what they
thought had happened to Barry, but Jillian knew
what they thought: that Barry had wandered away
in the night, that he had fallen down or become
frightened or lost something and was now out there
in the woods somewhere, dead.

But Jillian knew that Barry was not wandering
around lost, and she was sure he was not dead.
She just had to wait and hope 'they' would bring
him back to her. And so she was waiting . . . and
hoping . . . and praying. That was why she had
locked the doors and boarded up the windows and
taken the phones off their hooks. She didn't want
to talk to anyone – police, FBI, press, neighbours,
family or cranks, millions and millions of cranks.
She was waiting. For Barry. For a sign. For a
signal.

To help her get through this waiting period, to
help her keep her sanity, Jillian knew she had to
paint. So she had set up her easel and her paints in
a corner of the living room under a floor lamp –
the light wasn't very good, but it would have to do –

and for the past week she had been hard at it. Fourteen, fifteen, sixteen hours a day.

And always the same picture over and over again. A mountain, not a range of mountains, with valleys and canyons, but just this one mountain. With harshly grained sides. With outcroppings of trees and brush. She must have painted twenty, no, thirty different but similar pictures by now. Jillian did not find her behaviour obsessive. Not even unusual. She was going to keep on painting that mountain until she got it right – whatever that meant – or until she got a signal about Barry.

And so, Jillian Guiler listened to the men ringing the door bell and pounding on the doors and scratching at the windows, without really hearing anything. They would go away soon, they always did. And Jillian kept on painting the mountain.

SEVENTEEN

It was near Huntsville, Texas, in an abandoned sheetmetal factory, where all hell was busting loose. The vast floor space was overloaded with semi-trailer trucks and work crews speedily and efficiently loading them. The cargo was a strange collection of boxes, cartons, and crates. The smaller items arrived on conveyor belts, larger ones by fork lift, In one corner, men in stainless lab coats were packing metal canisters into Styrofoam-lined cases all marked *Special Handling*. A line of olive-drab jeeps waited on standby to trundle aboard. They bore no markings. Nor did the fibreglass modules that sat in the centre of the square next to a thousand feet of unassembled spidery metal scaffolding.

A Volkswagen bus pulled into the warehouse and Lacombe got out, followed by Laughlin and Robert. Aides rushed around behind and unloaded some simple Samsonite luggage.

'Is there anything Mr. Lacombe wants from his luggage?' an aide asked Laughlin. 'We want to get it on the airplane just as quickly as possible.' Lacombe understood most of the question and smiled a 'no, thank you', continuing a tour of the mobilization all around him. Laughlin looked worried. After all, the Frenchman had been active without sleep for over thirty hours so far.

'I have excitement inside!' Lacombe told his interpreter. 'Sleep will come when the excitement stops.'

Laughlin considered what little he already knew, and envisioned his employer awake for another ninety-six hours.

In another corner, away from the noisy activity, two dozen truckdrivers clustered around the dispatcher's desk. They were a motley group, some peeling off military uniforms and donning work-clothes and watch caps. The dispatcher was a no-nonsense lieutenant colonel with a very big stick. He used it to point at a mammoth map of the continental United States. The truckers pressed close and chewed gum.

'You heavy cargo people are going straight in. Use the bypass routes marked on your interstate maps. The rest of you will receive alternate route assignments just as soon as we finish collecting information on weigh stations along your way. Now, we're staggering you Peterbuilts. We don't want you all coming in together. And I'm going to ask you one more thing. Stay off the CB's and no unscheduled stop-overs. If any of you have to "go pottie," well, you know what to do.'

Above the din, a group of men stared at each other over coffee and cigarettes. They were in shirtsleeves and looked frazzled. Major Walsh circled the table and looked over the railing docks, the machinery, and all the noise. Walsh had never fancied home-front responsibility. This was his first year back from Special Forces Operations, both surface and clandestine in Tanzania, Zaire and Angola. And now, saddled with a security problem, Walsh was fighting mad that the Team Leader had drawn the line and not told him . . . everything. Walsh took a hit of coffee grounds and

Chesterfield Long before kicking a wastepaper basket halfway across the landing.

'You can't sell me an earthquake alert,' he snarled, sucking his cigarette down to the finger-tip. 'There's never been such a thing. These are ranchers – sheep and cattle and Indians. They don't live in high-rise condominiums.'

An exhausted-looking think-tanker rung his hands out and bent back in his chair. 'I still like the flash flood,' he yawned.

'Where you gonna get the water, pal?' said some-one else.

'We'll do a survey on dams and reservoirs in the watershed area. Tell 'em one's going to burst.'

Major Walsh tucked in his shirt and tightened his Disneyland bicentennial souvenir belt.

'We don't have time for a survey. You people know that. You should know that by now.'

Another guy, who had been attempting to break some sort of a record by contorting his Spidel Twist-o-Flex eleven times, coughed and interrupted.

'What about disease? You know, a plague epidemic?'

His buddy brightened at this and put down his pipe cleaning kit. 'Anthrax,' he bubbled. 'Isn't there a lot of sheep up there in Wyoming?'

Major 'Wild Bill' Walsh lit an Individuale and sat down.

'That's good,' he exhaled. 'But I'm worried it won't evacuate everyone. There's always a joker who thinks he's immune. I want something scary enough to clear three hundred square miles of every living Christian soul.'

At the heart of the confusion below, Lacombe

watched several workmen hoisting giant decals onto the bare silvery sides of the trailers. The decals read Piggly-Wiggly Supermarkets. Coca-Cola, Kenner Shoes, Folger's Coffee, and Baskin-Robbins 31 Flavors. Craving something sweet, the Frenchman popped a Listermint into his mouth and grinned at the American way of life. Then, the steel doors opened, someone yelled 'Westward Ho!' and the push was on.

EIGHTEEN

'No, Mother,' Ronnie was saying into the telephone, 'I can handle it. But thanks, anyway.'

She had cradled the phone between her ear and her shoulder while she stood in front of the kitchen stove, stirring pots.

Ronnie turned partway around, covered the mouthpiece of the phone with her free hand, and said to Toby, 'Go tell your father dinner's almost ready.'

Toby hesitated and then just stood where he was in the kitchen doorway, watching and listening to his mother.

'You're not helping me, Mother. You're not helping. We have Master Charge till the end of the month. He hasn't seen a doctor. He hasn't seen anybody.'

Ronnie turned and peered out the kitchen window. Roy was sitting in his patio chair on the platform he had built on top of the garage roof. The binoculars were jammed against his eyes as he slowly turned his head from side to side, sweeping the horizon.

'Yes, he's looking,' she told her mother. 'He's looking all the time, but not for work. I'm doing that . . . for me, Mother. Of course he loves us.'

Ronnie nodded her head vigorously and then had to grab the phone to keep it from falling. She noticed Toby still standing in the doorway. 'Toby, call your father for dinner ... You're not helping me, Mother ...'

The young boy moved slowly, almost unwillingly.

'Mother, I have to hang up now,' Ronnie said, and promptly did so.

She could hear Toby's thin voice outside the house. It was almost as if he were afraid to raise it because he was worried about being overheard by the neighbours.

'Dad, Mom's got dinner ready.'

Ronnie turned back to the window. Roy didn't seem to hear Toby calling. He didn't seem to hear anybody these days. Mrs. Harris from next door steered her car into the adjoining driveway and got out. Roy didn't hear that either, nor the disgusted plosive Mrs. Harris felt impelled to utter each time she found him on his lookout perch.

'Please, Dad,' Toby whimpered.

His father let the binoculars drop to his lap. He stared down through the gathering dusk at his youngest son. Even through the kitchen window Ronnie could see that Roy's face was damp. He must have been crying behind the binoculars. She thought of going out there to him, but then decided against it turning everything on the stove down to a low flame.

After a while, Neary climbed down. He came into the kitchen and stared at her for a moment. Ronnie saw that he'd dried his red-rimmed eyes. She also saw the prickly beginnings of a beard. Neary looked wiped out and, without a word, he moved past her into the family room on the way to the dining area.

Neary stopped at his miniature train layout,

fixating on a little brown mountain built into the middle of the Lilliputian countryside. He picked up some shrubs and moved them to the top of the model mountain, which he'd reconstructed into a tall peak with deeply ridged sides. He felt his guts sicken as his brain drained him of every ounce of energy while working to make sense of the mountain image.

'It's not right,' he said in a flat whisper, and left the room.

Since dinner was going to be delayed, Ronnie opened the refrigerator and put the bowl of salad back inside. The green bulb she had screwed into the socket turned all the food inside to unappetising shades of grey-green. She made a face at the stuff. What had seemed a great idea just a couple of weeks ago now seemed trivial and silly in the face of her own husband's unreasonable state of mind. Ronnie closed the refrigerator door quickly.

When Neary showed up for dinner, he'd neither washed nor changed. Ronnie noticed that the children seemed to edge away from him. She always sat at the opposite end of the table from Roy, but now the children seemed to cluster nearer to her end, than his, too uncomfortable with him to say anything.

She served and passed him his plate of salmon croquettes, niblet corn and mashed potatoes, with a square of margarine melting in the centre of the mound. He stared down as if no one had ever told him what to do with food on a plate.

Ronnie realized that the children were watching Roy intently as he started moving the mashed potatoes around the plate with his fork. He moulded the potatoes into a little peak. 'Not big enough,' he said. With a single back and forth motion he flicked the croquette onto the tablecloth.

The children were stunned.

Neary reached half-way across the table and took the serving bowl of mashed potatoes. He heaped a gob onto his plate, shaping it into a large mound. Neary froze to survey the situation. Not right! Another gob from the serving bowl. Not yet! So another, and one more until the bowl had been cleaned. Then, like a mad potter, Neary started to knead the white mush with his hands into some kind of shape.

Ronnie was trying to catch her breath, and Neary looked up at his family. They were frozen in place, staring at him. Roy wanted to talk to them; he wanted to touch them and make everything all right.

He forced a smile, then tried to make a funny face about himself.

'By now you've noticed,' he said, starting to laugh at his own understatement, 'something funny about Dad. Don't worry, I'm still Dad.'

Neary reached out to touch Sylvia, but she moved still further away from him toward her mother.

He tried again, addressing all the children. 'It's like when you know the music but you just don't get the words? I don't know how to say it, what I'm thinking ...' Neary pointed to the large mound of mashed potatoes. 'But ... this means something ... this is important.'

Roy looked up at Ronnie, who was concentrating on control. His mouth moved. 'I'm all right,' he was saying silently. 'I'm all right.' But no words came out.

Then Neary got to his feet and left the room.

The children's eyes swung back toward their mother.

Saddened, she said grimly, 'Let's eat,' and began forking the croquette into her mouth.

They all heard the shower start up, but they also heard over the running water the hacking, choking sounds of a man crying.

Ronnie stood up. 'Stay here,' she ordered the children, and left the room.

She listened at the bathroom door for a moment, then knocked twice, softly. Sweetheart ... Roy, please open the door.'

There was no answer, just the terrible coughing sobs. Ronnie tried the door handle. It turned but the door was locked. She stood there, her hand on the knob. 'Roy!' she called. Loudly this time. 'Roy!'

He didn't respond; he probably couldn't hear her.

Ronnie made a decision. She ran into the kitchen and got a butter knife out of the utensil drawer. 'Finish your dinner,' she shouted to the kids as she headed back toward the bathroom.

Ronnie knew what to do. At one time or another, all the children had locked themselves in their bedroom or bathroom. She fitted the butter knife between the door and the frame and gently eased the lock open. Then she turned the knob and pushed the door. It swung in.

The bathroom was dark. Water was pouring into the sink and the bathtub was half full, water smashing down into it from the showerhead. Neary was huddled in the far corner of the darkness, his hands mashed over his mouth to keep the sobs inside. Ronnie turned off the sink faucets, but left the shower running.

Neary tried to smile at his wife. His convulsions subsided slowly. 'It's like the hiccups,' he said in a small, childish voice. 'I started and I can't stop. What's happening to me?'

'All right, Roy,' Ronnie said, holding herself together. 'Mother gave me the name of this man. He's a doctor.'

'I'm scared to death,' he said, 'and I don't know why.'

Neary got up and sort of lunged over to the shower. He stuck his head under the spray. When he pulled out, Ronnie turned the faucets off and handed him a towel. She wanted to go over and hug his tears away, but she was too frightened. Another spasm of silent crying vibrated through Neary. After it passed, he opened the door of the medicine cabinet, somehow managed to get the lid of an aspirin bottle open and, with trembling hands, got two pills out and into his mouth. Then he dropped the bottle into the sink. It smashed.

'Look,' Ronnie said, trying to sound calm, reasonable. 'What he does is family therapy. We all go. You're not singled out. And maybe it's not your fault anyway.'

'I think maybe it's all a joke,' Neary said brokenly. 'Except look how I'm not laughing.'

'Roy! Say you'll go see him. You've got to promise me,' Ronnie told him, realizing that she was speaking to her husband in the same way that she dealt with her children when they were wrong. 'Promise?'

Suddenly the bathroom door was thrown open the rest of the way and Brad hurtled into the room. 'You crybaby!' he screamed at the image of his broken-down father. 'Crybaby! Crybaby!'

Brad tore out of the bathroom and hurtled toward his own room. He slammed his door five times, wanting to smash it off its hinges.

'You know he doesn't mean that. It's only, for him you're always so strong.'

Ronnie helped Roy into their bedroom. He had now stopped crying, but his trembling only intensified as he collapsed on their bed.

'I don't need a doctor,' he told her. 'I need you.'

Ronnie had no idea how to deal with this. She beat on the bedspread with her tiny fists. 'I can't help you,' she cried. 'I don't understand!'

'Neither do I.'

'All this nonsense is turning this house upside down,' she said, knowing this was no help at all.

'I'm scared,' Neary said, grabbing her right hand.

Ronnie tried to pull her hand free, but he wouldn't let go.

'I hate you like this,' she hissed as panic began to overtake her.

Roy reached out and pulled her down onto the bed.

'Hug me,' he said. 'That's all you have to do. Hold onto me . . . you can really help now.'

Ronnie pushed herself away. 'None of our friends call here anymore,' she complained, not looking down at him. 'You're out of work . . . you don't care! Roy, don't you understand, don't you see?' she cried out in a burst of panic. 'You're wrecking us!'

Neary reached up again and folded his wife into his arms. His trembling seemed to pulsate right through, and Ronnie suddenly knew that she was really incapable of bearing up to all this.

'Oh, don't,' she sobbed. 'Oh, don't. Let me call someone. Oh, Roy . . . please don't.'

But his fingers ripped at her clothing.

'I hate you, I hate you, hate you,' she sobbed, hating what he was doing to her.

Neary gripped the blouse at her shoulders and pulled. It ripped and the tattered ends pinned Ronnie's arms to her sides. He pulled the brassiere straps off her shoulders and slid the thing down her stomach, and then he slid down to her breasts and . . .

Almost immediately his anxiety flowed out of him. He cocked his head to the side and stared down at her silhouetted breasts.

Ronnie started to tremble then, her teeth chattering, silent sobs racking her body. She was helpless and horrified, but Neary was pulling something out of this for himself. Something constructive!

His mind raced on. No solution yet, but close. He could sense just how close. And, Jesus, he suddenly realized Ronnie had a beautiful body.

NINETEEN

In Denver, the evening was cold and clear. The thin air whistled around the CB antenna of the immense semi-trailer as it started the long haul down the sloping highway to the north. It flashed by in the dusk, its gigantic trailer blazing red for a moment in the last rays of the setting sun. FOLGER'S COFFEE, the sign ran along its high aluminium flank.

The Piggly-Wiggly trucks, two of them were already twenty miles east of Oakland and picking up speed on U.S. 580. Ahead, lay Altamont Pass, over 2,000 feet high.

The sun wasn't as far down on the horizon behind them as it was in Denver. The drivers were hoping to make Tracy by dark and then to bore on through, filling the night with noise and diesel exhaust as they shoved their cargo toward the setting sun.

It was dark by now on Interstate 80 running southeast out of Boise. The great semi with its powerful diesel engine dragging the trailer along at sixty-five miles per hour, headed toward Hammett and Mountain Home, Idaho. The trailer bore the brightly lettered name and design of Kinner Shoes, but in the darkness the name was almost invisible, except when passing cars' headlights slanted by.

The truck trailer pulled in for refuelling at a truck stop just east of Billings, Montana, where Interstate 90 ducks down through a corner of the

Big Horn National Recreation Area. The two drivers would have liked to stop for coffee, but their schedule didn't permit it. They'd have to be through the Custer Battlefield monument and into Sheridan, Wyoming by midnight.

The man pumping the diesel fuel looked up at the side of the truck. 'Never saw that one before,' he said.

The drivers and the gas jockey stared up at the lettering on the side of the trailer. TIDEWATER HOMES OF VIRGINIA.

'Kinda far from home, aren't ya?'

One driver wiggled his eyebrows. Of the two, he was the more communicative.

TWENTY

Neary hadn't really slept much at all. He'd kept Ronnie awake on and off. When he heard her breathing grow deeper, at about five in the morning, he eased himself out of bed and went into the family room.

Roy stared around the room with reddened eyes. He'd really wrecked the place during the last few days. Clippings from newspaper accounts of UFO sightings and the mysterious blackout were tacked here and there along the walls .

Neary groaned to himself and sat down in a chair, his elbow on the ping pong table, where the model railroad layout – an island of neatness and order in his otherwise insane world – awaited him. The odd peak that Neary had built up, more like a caricature of a mountain now, loomed grotesquely over the tracks and little lakes and valleys, ungainly, menacing.

Neary stared at it and shook his head. 'Not right,' he muttered.

'Daddy?'

He turned to see his little daughter, Sylvia, eyes half-mast with sleep. She had wandered out of her room, still trailing her favourite doll. The one that peed.

'Honey, it's so early,' Roy said. 'You should be asleep.'

'Daddy, are you going to yell at us some more today?'

Neary gazed down into her clear, guileless eyes. That was how he looked to her – a yelling machine. And she was prepared to accept more yelling because she loved him.

Neary felt his insides turn over with remorse. What a shit he was!

He leaned down and picked her up. 'I'm O.K. now, sweetheart.' Roy kissed his daughter on her forehead. He thought he might start crying again, but held himself together.

'O.K., Daddy.'

He glanced miserably around the room.

'I'm finished with all of this. Swear to God. Finished.'

Neary put the child back down and began pulling the clippings and photos down off the wall. 'Look at me,' he said, stuffing them in a wastebasket. 'Watch me now.'

Sylvia didn't know what he was talking about, but seemed happy that her father was happy.

Neary began tugging at the absurd mountain that he had built in the middle of the model railroad layout. He grabbed hold of the peculiar-looking peak and started yanking it. The mountain refused to budge and Neary, using two hands now, wrenched the thing sideways.

Snap!

The top section broke off, leaving the mountain truncated, as if some dreadnought had lopped off the peak, leaving a kind of plateau.

'Sylvia!' Neary shouted.

'Yes, Daddy?'

Roy's eyes were fixed on the strangely-broken peak. 'Sylvia,' he cried. '*That's right*!'

144

It was no way for anybody to wake up.

Ronnie had slept late, utterly wiped out by the events of the previous night, by Roy's breakdown and by her own inability to be anything much more than a chest for him to cry on.

Now it was ten in the morning and what had wakened her was the high, shrill cackle of her children. She listened for a moment and realized that all her family was laughing. Roy, too. Groggily, Ronnie thought she saw a bush go past the bedroom window.

She struggled out from under the covers and threw on a robe, tying the belt as she moved out of the bedroom and into the ki—

'Oh, my God,' Ronnie gasped.

The family room window was wide open, the screen removed, a ladder placed outside against the wall. As she watched, a hydrangea bush came hurtling through the window in a spray of thick, black dirt. It fell onto a huge pile of ... of other bushes, more dirt.

'Roy!'

Ronnie rushed to the kitchen door in time to see Brad and Toby uproot an azalea bush and sling it to their father, who ran up the ladder with the azalea and shoved it through the window into the den.

'Stop it!' Ronnie cried.

'C'mon, men,' Roy called to his sons. He seemed happier than Ronnie could remember seeing him in weeks, since the blackout.

Toby gave a cheer and began helping his father throw dirt through the window.

'After this can we throw dirt in my room?' he asked Roy.

'Stop it!' Ronnie cried. 'Stop it!'

She came running outside, acutely aware that Mrs. Harris was watching the whole thing from her second-floor window. A neighbour across the street had paused in the midst of mowing his grass and, transfixed like a cement lawn statue, stood open-mouthed staring. Ronnie knocked the dirt out of Toby's hands and confronted her husband.

'I'm going to make that phone call' she told him. 'We can be there in an hour.'

'If I don't do this,' Neary said, still pitching dirt through the window, 'I *will* need a doctor'

'Do what? What are you doing?'

'Ronnie, I figured it out. Have you ever looked at something one way and it looks crazy, then you look from another way and it makes perfect sense? No!!'

'Roy, you're scaring us!'

The force of Ronnie's statement did scare the children a little. Neary had been yanking at a geranium. He looked up suddenly, as if seeing his wife for the first time. 'Don't be scared, honey. I feel good. Everything's going to be all right.'

He gave up on the geranium as his eye caught sight of a small aluminium patio table. Picking it up, Neary pitched it through the den window. It made almost no sound on landing, its impact cushioned by the layers of dirt and bushes on the floor inside.

'Don't tell me everything is going to be all right,' Ronnie screamed after him, 'while you're throwing the yard into the den.'

Roy ran around to the front of the yard. Now he had his eye on two large green plastic trash cans that were standing at the end of the driveway. A sanitation truck was just pulling up and two garbage collectors were about to leap off the truck to empty Neary's cans. Roy accelerated and beat them to the cans, grabbing and emptying them on the sidewalk, then rushing back toward the house. He flew past Ronnie and the children, leaving two piles of garbage and two amazed garbage men in the driveway.

Moving like a high-hurtler, knees up, he hotfooted it back to the house, a container in each hand, throwing them through the window into the family room where they bounced off the patio table and rolled off the geranium balls and peat moss.

Suddenly, Roy was struck with a new thought. 'Chicken wire,' he said aloud.

Ronnie watched him hurdle the low ornamental fence that separated their driveway from the one next door. A roll of chicken wire stood in the open doorway of the Harris' garage. Mrs. Harris stuck her head out the window as Neary picked up the roll of wire and started to take it away.

'Whatever you're doing,' Mrs. Harris said wildly, 'is against the law.'

'He's putting it back, Mrs. Harris,' Ronnie called to her desperately.

She had gathered the two boys to her side, somehow communicating without words that the fine maniac frenzy of helping their father was terminated. Frightened now, Brad and Toby clung to Ronnie's robe, watching the scene play out.

'I'll pay for it,' Neary called up to Mrs. Harris.

'Take it! Take it!' Mrs. Harris brandished her

hot air blower at Roy like a revolver.

Now the baby, Sylvia, started to wail but Neary didn't seem to hear. He tossed the roll of wire through the window into the house and began foraging the yard for more material. Ronnie, with all three children clinging to her now, managed to get in his path.

'Roy, I'm taking the kids to my mother's house,' She was crying now.

Neary had been moving at top speed. Abruptly, his forward motion was checked. He nearly pitched over as he braked to a halt. 'That's crazy,' said the voice of reason. 'You're not dressed.'

'That's what?' Ronnie shrieked. 'You said what?'

Now it was her turn to move fast. Carrying Sylvia and sweeping the boys along by the sheer force of personality, Ronnie hurried them all to the car.

'Wait!' Roy shouted, going after them.

She shoveled all the kids into the station wagon, then turned to him, saying, 'I've done that.' Ronnie rolled up all the windows and powerlocked the doors.

'Ronnie,' he called to her through the safety glass. 'Please stay here! Please be with me now.'

'For what?' her voice sounding muffled. To Neary it seemed as though she were already fading away. 'To see them take you away in a strait-jacket?'

Roy started banging on the doors and windows of the wagon, Ronnie started the engine and jammed the car in reverse.

Neary stopped banging, but leaped on the hood of the car as Ronnie began backing it out of the driveway through the piles of left-over garbage. He could see his children's eyes widen with terror, watching their father pounding his fists on the hood and yelling. Then, as Ronnie backed faster down the driveway, he had to hold onto the radio antenna with one hand to keep from sliding off.

Ronnie hated this now. She wheeled back hard out of the driveway into the street, stopped abruptly, throwing Roy off the hood and onto the sidewalk, and then curled her toes around the accelerator pedal and blasted off down the street, around a corner and was gone.

Neary lay on the sidewalk, more stunned than hurt, in his filthy pyjamas. Slowly, starting to hurt a little from his fall, he got to his feet. He looked up and noticed for the first time that a half a dozen of his friends and neighbours had witnessed the whole thing and were hanging in for a socko finish of some kind. Neary wondered what they were expecting. Chimes?

'Morning!' he called to the crowd, waving at them all.

Then Neary turned and strode magnificently off along the grass to the window ladder. He stopped to pick up the garden hose and turned on the water. Then, trotting up the ladder with the hose, splashing water on himself and everything else, he climbed through the family room window, pulling the ladder up and in after him.

Once inside and with a majestic gesture, Roy slammed down the window and pulled the drapes, shutting out the neighbours and the entire outside world.

In the family room, the show continued for quite a while, fortunately out of anyone's sight but Neary's. He worked steadily at it all day with nothing to eat or drink and no human voice except the faint babble of the television set in the corner, lisping its daytime idiocies, blighted soap opera lives, shrieking game-show contestants, banal junk movies.

It really hadn't mattered to Neary what the television was doing. Inside the family room something much greater, something immense, was under way. He had gone to work like the trained engineer he was, shaping out of the empty garbage containers and the lawn table a kind of rough core or support for what he was constructing.

Then, with Mrs. Harris's chicken wire, he had created a contour less rough, more complex, to the thing he was building. And then, making a muddy paste of the dirt, he had plastered the chicken wire until he had it right.

Still not content, he'd wet down newspapers and smoothed them over the mud to form a kind of hard-edged papier-maché surface, stained with dirt, that uncannily resembled the surface of . . . of what he was making.

'It's not right yet,' he muttered unhappily around five in the afternoon.

He had built the thing from the floor up, braced it with uprooted bushes hidden inside the mud. It towered over him now, touching the ceiling nine feet overhead. Its sloping sides were striated in angry ridges. But he wasn't fully satsified – not yet.

Neary caught sight of the landscaping on the model railroad. He snatched up miniature trees and shrubs. Holding them like chess pieces, he took his time figuring their proper placement. Just so. Here two pines. Exactly. And there a line of bushes. Precisely there.

'Right,' he said at last. 'Finally, it's right.'

He'd barely had time to think of what he was doing – didn't remember, for instance, that he'd had three dry runs on this project, once with a pile of shaving cream, once in the dirt of State 57 when little Barry had first sculpted this strange, conical peak, once with the entirely unsatisfactory mashed potatoes.

But he had it now. It could pass for the real thing, Neary told himself. Now that the mud had dried over the stiffening surface of newspapers, it really looked real, especially with the trees and shrubbery in place.

The fluted walls rose sharply to a kind of plateau at the top, a mesa-like place. Around on one side lay a box canyon in which a peaceful Shangri-la Valley was shaded by more of the model railroad greenery.

Neary had been breathing hard all day. Now, as he stood there, slowly circling his creation, inspecting it for flaws and finding none, his breathing began to slow to a calm, peaceful tempo. He felt at ease now for the first time since he'd been seized by the need to ... to *make this thing*.

He paused and squinted at the mesa top. Beyond it, through a window, he could see the normal life of the neighbourhood outside. A car stopped and some people emerged, walked up to a neighbour's house and were greeted at the open front door. His other middle-class neighbours were mowing and pruning and watering. Cars moved by. Children played.

Normality.

Neary shoved filthy fingers through his hair and stared hard at the mountain towering over him. He had made it. It had cost him, but he had made it. It was supposed to mean something, wasn't it?

But now that he'd sacrificed so much to it, there it stood. Meaning nothing.

'My God,' Neary said out loud. 'It's only me. Oh, my God, it's only me.'

It was the low point of his life, and to make matters worse, the silly, plastic normality of the TV sitcoms now arrived.

Not really listening to them, Neary slumped down in an armchair, staring at the flat topped pinnacle he had created and that had cost him so much.

He didn't actually watch the television as it ground through hours of reruns. He let it exist as a form of radio, giving him only the thin semi-human voices that trickled from its tiny speaker. Reruns.

Gomer Pyle was chewed out by his Sergeant not once but twice. Lucy got caught by her boss taking an extra hour for lunch. Rustlers invaded the Ponderosa, setting fires. On the stand the witness broke down under Perry Mason's questioning and confessed. Robert Young performed open-heart surgery in a power blackout.

About nine-o'clock Neary stirred, went to the refrigerator and took out a beer. He popped it open. Surgery in a blackout, he thought. He blinked, put down the open can of beer and went to the telephone to dial a number.

'Let me talk to her,' he said after a minute.

When Ronnie came on the line, he cleared his throat carefully. 'Don't you think I'm worth it? Just don't hang up, Ronnie . . . Oh, please don't—'

Then he heard the click.

'Madge, tell me, how do you get your cakes so moist and fluffy?'

'Now I feel safe, safe, even with nervous perspiration.'

Neary still wasn't watching the tube, but the flow of commercial pap had begun to filter more directly into his hearing. He was still examining the . . . what could he call it? – the mountain.

'. . . crispy-good and just this much oil left in each one!'

Neary stirred and went to the telephone again. He dialled Ronnie's mother. 'Put her on, please.'

'Roy, I'm sorry, she doesn't want to talk to you.'

'Put her on!' he shouted.

He waited. The line was still open. He held the phone in one hand and stared through the kitchen doorway into the family room.

He waited. No one came to the phone, neither Ronnie nor her mother. He strained to hear anything over the line, sounds of argument, anything. But it was still open. When he blew into the mouthpiece, he still got what phone technicians called 'side tone.'

So she hadn't hung up. So there was hope. The minutes went by. He eyed the kitchen clock. One minute to ten. As if it had been planned for that moment, he heard someone softly hang up the phone at Ronnie's mother's house. He cursed and redialled the number.

Busy signal. She'd taken it off the hook.

He picked up the beer and wandered back into the family room as the ten o'clock news came on. A man with the fashionably fluffed hair that hides his ears stared meaningfully into the lens of the camera, his eyes barely moving as he read the words off the Teleprompter screen.

'Good evening! Top of the news tonight ... rail disaster!' To Neary the man seemed to bite off the words nourishing something in the announcer's soul.

'A chemical gas derailment,' the man was saying, 'has forced the widest area evacuation in the history of these controversial Army-rail shipments. The remote area of Devil's Tower, Wyoming is the scene of this latest mishap. Charles McDonnell is on the scene for a live report.'

Neary's eyes began to glaze, but he continued to watch the TV screen. McDonnell, in a trenchcoat, stood with the mike in his hand. Behind him trucks were moving down a road while in the distance, mountain peaks stood against the sky.

'It's sundown here in the hot zone of Wyoming,' McDonnell said, 'and thousands of civilian refugees are fleeing the scene of disaster. Seven tank cars of the dangerous G-M nerve gas, destined for destruction by chemical means under safe conditions, overturned a few hours ago at Walkashi Needles Junction.

'There are no real towns or settlements in these wild Wyoming foothills,' he went on, 'but vacation camps and cottages are being evacuated now as Army and Marine trucks and helicopters comb an area one hundred miles in diameter that has as its centre the peak known as Devil's Tower.'

The camera pulled back to show the cortege of

trucks moving past. Then, with a blink, the picture changed to a telephoto shot of a distant mountain peak.

'The steep sides of Devil's Tower,' McDonnell was saying, 'have made it a testing ground for mountain climbers from all over the world who—'

'Jesus!'

Neary was on his feet. In one jump he knelt before the television screen. There it was, the same mountain he had just finished making. There it was on the screen. There it was in his family room.

The same. The fluted sides. The flat mesa top. The trees, in the same positions. He stared at the screen, then at the model he had made, then back at the screen.

'Ronnie!' he yelled. 'Ronnie! I'm not crazy!'

A huge grin split his face as he raced for the telephone in the kitchen. His finger slipped twice while dialing. He had to stop, hang up and start all over again. He felt a fine trembling in his body.

It had meant something. It hadn't been some sort of lunacy. He didn't know what it was all about yet, but he knew that the urge, the terrible compulsion to build, had a meaning. It wasn't the random insanity of a sick mind.

It was a message.

Forcing himself to slow down, he dialled the number correctly.

And got the same busy signal.

The smile left his face. He turned toward the den and stared at the model he had created of Devil's Tower. It was a hell of a long way west of Indiana, he thought, a hell of a trip to take, alone and wondering.

Neary stared blankly at the open phone book. Idly, he flipped its pages. Then he began paging more carefully until he got to the listings for Harper Valley. Gold. Gowland. Guber. Guiler, J.

He dialled Jillian's home. Earlier, when he'd called to find out about Barry, all he'd got was a busy signal.

'I *am* sorry,' a recorded voice told him this time. 'Your call *cannot* go through as dialled. Please *hang* up and dial again. This *is* a recording. I *am* sorry. Your c—.'

He dialled again and got the same recording.

It was going to be a long trip to take, but he'd have to do it alone.

Jillian Guiler had not left the house all these days. Except to lie down to sleep, use the bathroom and eat an occasional, erratic snack, Jillian had not really left the living room or her paintings.

She did not look at all well. She had lost a lot of weight since Barry had been taken. More than that, though, Jillian had the look of someone who had suffered the greatest loss imaginable and was paying for it.

The corner of the living room where she had spent her days and nights resembled a deranged art gallery of heavily charcoaled and ruthlessly coloured canvasses of a mountain that had taken on many of the aspects of Roy Neary's mad creation.

Sometime during the past week, Jillian had turned on the television set, although she, too, hardly watched or listened. Now, however, her attention had been grabbed. By the evening news. She had tuned to a different station from Neary.

Then by the magic of television Jillian got her first look at Devil's Tower.

'The army and National Guard units are supervising the evacuation. Dislocated families have been assured that the danger will have passed within seventy-two hours, once the toxin concentration is down to fifty parts per million. This means most residents will be back in their own homes by the weekend ... of course, this is small consolation to livestock in the area, although ranchers have been notified that the quality of meat should remain unaffected. That means order that steak "well-done", Walter ...'

A commercial came on and Jillian fell backward against her drawings. There was the tower again seen from the same angle as the television camera. The difference being that in her charcoal sketches there were no Huey helicopters perambulating the woodlands at the base of the gigantic peak. She stood rooted to the spot for so long that the network news ended and *The Hollywood Squares* began. Jillian picked herself up and took the pieces into the bathroom. Moving with small, deft gestures, like a repairman meticulously reassembling a watch. Jillian showered, did her hair, put on makeup, packed, and left the house. She prayed that she was on her way to Barry now.

A man who hasn't slept for a couple of days, Neary told himself, shouldn't have to go through all this. He felt shaky, but determined that the details of it were going to stay within his control.

He badly needed the car Ronnie had taken, but that couldn't be helped. Neither could the lack of sleep. He showered and shaved, which did help. But by eight in the morning, the false feeling of well-being had evaporated. He started walking to the centre of town.

The situation, he told himself, is far from hopeless.

Neary had been carrying twenty dollars in his wallet. He had found another twenty Ronnie usually hid away at the back of the freezer where a burglar wouldn't look. Neary had also, with some pangs of guilt, looted Brad's piggy bank of four dollars and change.

By eight-thirty he was at the savings bank, drawing out forty dollars of the forty-two dollars and seventeen cents on deposit there. By nine he was at the commercial bank, shoving across to the teller a cheque for a hundred dollars. After consulting the account balance, the teller shoved the cheque back to Neary.

'Sorry. Would you like to see our loan officer over th—?'

Neary tore the cheque to bits the size of confetti and strode out of the bank. Damned bad luck. Then he saw the liquor store across the street. Hope! He flung the confetti into the air with a holiday gesture.

With that grudging combination of suspicious civility and terrible slowness that comes from not really wanting to do something, the liquor store manager nevertheless cashed the cheque. 'You're running me out of twenties, Mr. Neary,' was his only complaint.

The nine-fifteen bus brought Neary to Cincinnati by eleven. He got to the airport in time to present the reservation clerk with his problem. She consulted two directories, three lists and her supervisor before booking Neary on a through flight to Denver, a connection to Cheyenne, and a flight on a feeder airline with the improbable name of Coyote Airlines. She also reserved a rental car for Neary at his destination.

She seemed to be taking quite a while to do all this, but Neary didn't begin to get suspicious until he caught her glance moving past him to two guards standing a few feet to the rear.

Neary turned to face them. He could see they hadn't yet made up their minds if he'd 'flunked the profile' or not. Like all airport security people, they had been trained to recognize several types of potential troublemaker by a 'profile,' which described them in physical terms: dressed a certain way, looking a certain way, talking a certain way. Neary could tell they were on the brink of fitting him into one of the pigeonholes labelled 'potential hijacker' or 'terrorist.'

He turned back to the reservation clerk. 'Miss,' he said, 'Would you watch my things for a second? I'll be right back.'

Picking up his overnight case, Neary headed for the nearest men's room. The two guards followed but didn't go in with him. Inside, he lathered his face with soap and water, took a quick shave, changed to a medium-blue shirt, knotted a dark brown tie in place and carefully combed his hair.

He walked out of the men's room and passed within a yard of the two security men. Only one of them recognized him. Their glance followed Neary all the way back to the counter, but neither guard made a move.

Padding the 'profile,' Neary mused, was easier than it looked.

The money part of it was easy, too. Neary learned that a shower, a shave, fresh clothes and a Master Charge card leave no one in doubt as to a man's solvency.

Now for the hard part. He got an envelope and some paper from the ticket clerk, bought a stamp at the insurance counter and sat down. He had no idea where to begin. He killed time by addressing the envelope to Brad, Toby, and Sylvia Neary. Their names looked strange. He'd never written them a letter in his life.

'Dear kids. I'll be away a while. If I come ba—'

He blinked, scratched out the 'if' and continued writing. 'When I come back I'll have some story to tell. I have to do this. I have to find out and this is the only way to do it.'

His vision blurred. He found that his eyes had filled with tears. Brad had been right. He was a terrible crybaby. Neary glanced around, but no one was watching. He wiped his eyes and kept on writing.

'Boys, help your mother. You're good, reliable boys and—.' He stopped. Helluva lot more reliable than your old man, he thought.

'I should be home real soon and—.'

Not right to tell kids lies, Neary thought. He was disturbing them enough as it was. They probably hated him by now, or soon would. He had to make a better stab at explaining this. He owed them that much.

'None of this means much to you,' he wrote. 'Even less to your mother. But it's like the song

Jiminy Cricket sings. Did I ever take you to Pinocchio? I can't remember if we—.'

He rubbed his eyes. 'Everybody has a secret wish. I can't explain it. All I can say is that it's stronger than anything else. When you wish upon a star.'

The letter slipped off his knee and fell to the floor. Neary sat there, helpless, tears running down his cheeks. He stared bleakly at the letter as if it lay at the bottom of the sea, unreachable through miles of filmy, shifting currents.

Grunting with the effort, he bent down and picked up the letter. Without rereading it, he signed it 'love Dad' and rammed it into the envelope. He got up and moved slowly, like an old man, like a deep-sea diver in a heavy leaden suit, to the mailbox.

He dropped the letter in the box and stood there for a long time, staring. U.S. MAIL. U.S. MAIL USMAIL USMAIL.

When his flight was called over the loudspeakers, he was still standing there. The second time they announced boarding, Neary turned slowly from the mailbox. He straightened up a little. Then he marched off toward the waiting flight.

TWENTY-ONE

The Hertz Rent-A-Car station in this part of the world wasn't the usual sleek yellow-and-black office with a sleek young woman in her yellow-and-black uniform. In this part of Wyoming, the Hertz office was in Mutt's Garage and you had to look real hard to see the small yellow-and-black sign.

Apart from working on engines, Mutt hated every other part of running a garage. He hated pumping gas, fixing flats, replacing wiper blades and renting Hertz cars. And, to cap it off, he hated Roy Neary long before he ever laid eyes on him.

'Oh, *you're* Neary,' he said glowering. 'You took your sweet goddamned time gettin' here.'

'But you've got the jeep for me.'

'I got *a* car,' Mutt admitted grudgingly. 'They ain't no more jeeps this necka th'woods, Neary. You're goddamned lucky I was able to hold onto that sucker back there. Christ, I coulda rented her twenty times over in the last day.'

'People getting out of the area?' Neary asked.

' 'F wasn't fer that goddamned reservation you made in Cincinnati, I'd a rented the sucker and got the hell out same's everybody else. Sign here,' he added with no change in tone. 'Initial here and here. Where's your goddamned driver's licence? Awright.' He scribbled furiously on the rental agreement. 'Git.'

163

'I hardly expected such gracious treatment from—.'

'Beat it,' Mutt said. 'You gotta full tanka gas and that's the works. When you turn the sucker in, I won't be here. Just leave the keys in the goddamned ashtray.'

Mutt was already out the garage door ahead of Neary. He jumped into the driver's seat of a Ford pickup and disappeared in a great cloud of dust before Neary had even taken the keys from the counter.

Neary took his overnight bag and a copy of the rental agreement around the back to see what kind of sucker he'd rented. 'A Vega sucker!' he yelped, getting in and starting up the engine. He flipped on the radio.

'. . . thousands of others are homeless,' the announcer came in on cue. Obviously there was no other news in Wyoming but the evacuation story.

'The U.S. Army Materiel Command has issued these new restrictions. All roadways north of Crowheart on Interstate 25 . . . all roads leading into the Grand Teton west of Meetestse . . . all multi-lane, undivided full-traffic interchange, gravel, local and historic state roads north of Cody and east to Burlington, or west to Yellowstone Lake . . . all are now declared unsafe and included in the Red Zone. All are declared—.'

Neary switched off the radio and examined the road map he had picked up in Mutt's Garage when Mutt wasn't looking. He located the newly forbidden roads and traced them back in the Tetons to Devil's Tower.

He sat for some time considering his alternate

routes in. G-M nerve gas or no G-M nerve gas, he *was* going in.

At Reliance, under a cloudless blue sky, the day was perfect for a picnic.

Instead it was roundup time, not of beef cattle but of evacuees. For miles now, Neary had been aware he was the only car moving west into the Tetons. The lanes east were jammed with over-crowded vehicles. He'd hoped to gas up in Reliance and keep moving, but for the first time, he ran head-on into the military.

A roadblock had been thrown across the highway right at the railway station. National Guard soldiers, rifles slung across their backs, faces damp in the bright, hot sunlight, were herding people through what were normally feed and loading pens for cattle.

'Now boarding blue cards only,' a sergeant roared over a bullhorn. 'All evacuees with blue boarding cards move in quickly. Those with red cards shape up behind that barrier. You'll be next.'

He paused to clear his throat, hawk and spit without snapping off the bullhorn. The sounds echoed across the station area. 'Stay in line. You'll all get aboard. Just stay in line. Blue cards boarding now . . .'

He watched a corporal fully six and a half feet tall take note of the Vega and start to lumber over, a stubborn set to his heavy jaw. But before he could reach Neary, a mixed herd started through the roadblock.

Steers intermingled with spring sheep, making progress almost impossible. The rich aroma of manure lay over the scene. 'Git them woolly faggots outa my herd!' a steer rancher shouted.

'You leave them sheep be,' the owner of the flock warned him, 'or there'll be beef by-products from here to Jackson Hole.'

An Air Force chopper hovered over the milling cattle and managed to spook them into a mini-stampede that cleared the road block. Then the helicopter lifted sharply, like a rising balloon, and headed at once for the high Tetons.

Neary was watching it disappear in the direction he longed to go when the shadow of the man-mountain corporal fell on him. 'You got next-uh-kin in the red zone?' the soldier rumbled.

'Sue-Ellen, my baby sister,' Neary replied.

'Last name?' the corporal pulled out a clipboard with a list of names.

'Hennersdorfer.'

Slowly, moving the tip of a blunt finger like a snowplow down the sheets of names, the corporal made his way in and out of the 'H' range of the alphabet. 'No Hennersdorfer.'

'My God, then she's still in there!' Neary exclaimed.

'We got everybody out by noon yesterday.'

'Not Baby Sue-Ellen.'

'No way,' the implacable soldier told him. 'Everybody's out. We made a house-to-house. Ain't no Baby Sue Nobody in there.

'I gotta check it myself,' Neary said. 'Ma and Pa'd never forgive me if Baby Sue-Ellen was killed because I was too lazy to go in and bring her out of th—.'

'Hey,' the corporal cut in. 'You don't understand

English, do you? Everybody's outa there. Nobody's going in. And I got orders to shoot looters on sight. Get the message, Hennersdorfer?'

Neary grinned foolishly. 'See you.' He reversed the Vega and got out of there, but not before he heard the corporal talking with a buddy.

'Another scavenger, huh?' the buddy asked.

'Sweetheart,' the corporal bragged, 'I can smell 'em in a hurricane.'

Neary's smile narrowed slightly as he left the area of the railroad station. He wasn't a scavenger or a looter, but if anybody'd asked him his real motive for being there, he'd have no respectable answer. 'Researcher?' Or 'curious person?' Maybe . . . 'invited guest'.

More like it. Because whatever had given him the lunatic drive and energy to mow down every part of his normal life and build that insane nine-foot-high model of Devil's Tower, whatever had induced him to do that was sending him a message plain and clear. And whatever else the message said, it was an invitation to Devil's Tower.

The only problem was how to get there, now that he was within fifty miles of the place. Walking, he'd get lost or shot. Besides, he wasn't all that sure he could successfully escape the G-M nerve gas.

'Folks, I don't wish to alarm you,' a man was saying as Neary parked his car.

The man was skinny, bald, with a long upper lip and a wide mouth, a talker's mouth that liked words and used a lot of them. He had already collected a small crowd, but with the near-panic situation in Reliance, Wyoming, a crowd was the easiest thing in the world to collect.

'Let me tell you what you already know,' the man went on. 'G-M nerve gas is colourless and odourless. You won't have no idea in the wide world when you're breathing it or touching it, nosiree. But then,' he went on, warming to his speech, 'when your eyes begin to di-a-late and your nose starts a'running, you're gonna ask yourself: "Dear God, why didn't I buy myself one of them early warning systems the man told me about?" You're gonna wish you had.'

About thirty people were clustered around him now, 'And when that bloody discharge starts running from your nose and mouth,' the man continued, 'and your muscles seize up so's you embarrass yourself in your pants, you'll regret not taking this simple precaution, guaranteed sure, safe and certain.'

He held up a small cheap cage in which a dispirited yellow bird clung to a wooden dowel. 'This here canary gives you precisely one hour of sure, safe and certain early warning,' he said, 'and it's a godsend at fifty bucks.'

Neary got out of his car and walked across the street to join the crowd around the bird peddler. People were starting to shove money at him, which his wife took as he handed out caged canaries.

'Can't afford a canary?' he was asking in a high voice, his mouth working smoothly, easily as the words flowed, 'then I got you a special on doves. They give you a forty-five minute head start, not as much as a canary, but then, they don't cost no fifty bucks neither. Thirty dollars takes away a dove.'

Neary pushed toward the stacks of cages. 'Let

me have two canaries,' he said.

'Two's better'n one. A dove's better 'n nothing. And in the bargain basement I got chickens, twenty bucks a piece and they give you a whole half hour of warning.'

Neary fished in his pocket for money while, with the other hand, he reached across to take the two caged birds. Carrying them back to his car he was about to get in.

'Roy!'

He whirled around. 'Roy!' the woman's voice called again. He stared at the crowd pushing aboard the rescue train. Surely the voice came from there, but . . .

'Roy!'

He saw her then, struggling against the flow of people, trying to make her way out of the crowd toward him. Jillian.

All the nightmarishness of the place seemed to focus down on the two of them. They fought to close the gap between them, but swarms of people kept them apart.

Soldiers yelled through bullhorns. Sheep shoved past. Cars kept trying to move down the crowded main street. The bird peddler's spiel was a cry of anguish.

The sun flooded the scene with painful intensity.

'Over here!' Neary called. Jillian was in danger and didn't realize it. The crowd had started to shove hard in its anxiety about getting into the train. Going against them, she risked being shoved to the ground, trampled.

'Get off!' he shouted. 'Jump off the ramp!'

He waded through the crowd now, shoving people

aside. Jillian fought her way sideways, then half jumped, half fell from the ramp.

Neary caught her. They held each other tightly as people streamed by on both sides, children, cattle, people carrying bird cages, an old woman with a tortoise shell cat, a boy with a transistor radio glued to his ear, a man carrying two infants, a woman with four pillowcases crammed with possessions. The noise was frightening.

Jillian and Neary clung together, bodies pressed close. They were saying things they couldn't hear, babbling and laughing into each other's faces. Then Roy began to edge them sideways out of the crowd, through the line of steers moving along the sidewalk, and back to his car.

Jillian slumped down in the front seat and covered her eyes with her hand. Neary got behind the wheel and started the car. 'Hold onto the canaries,' he said as they moved off down the street. 'What the hell, I don't even think there really is poison gas out there. Do you?'

'Roy,' she moaned, 'I'm so happy it's you.'

'Me, too.' He laughed.

'And your children? Your wife?'

This time Neary was silent. He had driven out of Reliance by now, part of a long line of eastbound cars. He pulled over to the side of the road at an intersection blocked by a jeep and two National Guardsmen.

'No turns here,' one of them called. 'Keep moving?'

'Just taking a rest.' Neary turned to Jillian. 'They left me,' he said then. 'Ronnie and the kids took off. I was getting too flaky for them.'

170

Jillian's mouth twisted sideways. 'Flaky. That's what the F.B.I. man told me. I could see he didn't believe what I was telling him.'

Neary nodded. 'Listen, Jillian, we didn't both come out to Wyoming just to turn around and go back.'

'But they have the roads blocked.'

'There's a way. This is a big country. This is beer commercial country.'

She said nothing for a moment. Then she took his hand and brought it to her cheek. 'I'm glad we met again.'

Then, Neary spotted what he was searching for all along. A stretch of countryside protected by barbed wire and not much else. The barbed wire had begun to rust in places. Neary backed up the Vega for a running start. He downshifted into hill-climbing gear for more torque. He rammed the gas pedal down to the floor. Under the hood the engine roared. Rear wheels spouted Wyoming dust.

The grille slammed head on onto the fence. With a 'bwoinng!' like a guitar string, the barbed wire snapped.

TWENTY-TWO

Now the Vega was careening across empty brushland. Tyres popped up and down in potholes, wood-
chuck burrows, tiny valleys of erosion. Jillian had
strapped herself in and was holding the canaries on
her lap. Even so, she and the birds jounced up and
down sickeningly.

'The police dragged the river for him,' Jill started
again to get her mind off the air pockets. 'I told
them he wasn't in the river. He wasn't in the river!
They went around to every house for five miles
looking inside back yard refrigerators. Then they
asked me if I had seen any strangers in the neighbourhood. Oh, brother!'

Neary steered like a madman, whipping a wheel
left and right to avoid the bigger chuckholes, half
standing off the seat to see far enough ahead in
this wasteland so that he could anticipate what was
coming next.

There were no roads, not even cattle trails. All
he could hope was that his tyres and shock absorbers
would hold out long enough for them to reach the
base of Devil's Tower.

He could see it behind some intervening hills. He
could see everything. As he glanced around, he
could still see very faintly in the distance the long
highway of cars heading east. He wondered if anyone who had seen him swerve out of line and ram
the fence would take the trouble to report him to
one of the many National Guardsmen along the

route. He kind of doubted it.

In any event, here came something that seemed better than brushland. Neary tramped on the brakes, downshifted into low again, and rammed through another wire fence. The Vega shook its nose and dropped with a 'thunk' onto a gravel road heading directly for Devil's Tower.

Neary slowed under the shade of a stunted scrub pine and inspected the birds. They appeared dazed, but Neary couldn't determine whether it was cross-country nerves or something worse.

He drove off along the gravel stage trail at a slower pace. It began to lead to higher ground now, skirting the base of foothills, rising constantly. As the Vega rounded another corner—

They both saw it at the same time. The Vega seemed to roll to a stop, all by itself.

They got out of the car and walked to the edge of the embankment to stare at it – Devil's Tower, looking a mile high.

'Good God,' Jillian said.

'It's just I—' Neary stopped, moisted his lips. 'Just like I imagined it—' He stopped again, feeling that words could never express what he was feeling, the sense of *having got it right* at last, of having brought everything together so that, finally, it had begun to mean something.

The two of them stood silently before the awesome sight. Nothing nearby resembled this vision out of their dreams. The Tower stood alone, unique, something so one-of-a-kind that Neary felt a chill across his shoulders at the thought that he had been able to reproduce it in sculpture without even knowing it existed.

He cleared his throat. 'I guess we'd better move on,' he said then, 'or they'll spot us.'

Jillian's glance seemed to click downward for an instant. 'There,' she said, pointing to a place just ahead on the gravel road. 'Isn't that a gas station?'

After a few minutes Neary steered the car into the abandoned station, really nothing more than a cabin that sold souvenirs and snacks with a single gas pump out front. He lifted out the hose and shunted the cutoff lever. The pump growled. 'Still got electricity,' Neary muttered. He filled the Vega's tank and replaced the hose. 'Nine bucks,' he said under his breath.

'Roy.' He heard what Jillian was warning him about, the faraway beat of a helicopter rotor, moving closer. Neary pulled her out of the car and they stood in the doorway of the cabin, hoping the choppers would pass by without noticing them.

A squadron of transport Hueys cruising hazardously low zoomed over them. Flying somewhat higher than the rest were two flanking helicopters carrying clusters of chemical toilets from their undercarriage supports. Behind them a single Air Force Cheyenne hung protectively in the sky.

Abruptly, the Cheyenne shifted sideways and dropped like a plummet until it was just over the roof of the cabin. Before Neary could open the door and drag Jillian inside, one of the men in the copter, wearing goggles and some kind of breathing mask, picked up a Polaroid camera and aimed it at Neary and Jillian.

Neary shrugged and produced a grin. The photographer seemed to be racking his special lens for a zoom closeup. Neary stepped out of the doorway and into the sunlight. He dug in his pocket and produced a ten-dollar bill. Waving it at the helicopter, he walked over to the gas pump and laid the bill on top, weighing it down with a rock.

'Okay?' he called.

The only response was the pilot tapping the photographer on the arm. Then he sent the chopper ballooning into the sky. It headed off toward the direction of Devil's Tower, where the other copters had already disappeared from view.

'That does it,' Neary said. 'Hop in.'

He gunned the Vega up to seventy on the gravel road, taking the turns and twists on two wheels, ducking under tree cover whenever a helicopter appeared in the sky. At one point, waiting for a chopper to fly away, Neary saw a bird lying in the road, on its back, claws in the air. Silently, he pointed it out to Jillian.

'You want me to turn back?'

'What killed it, Roy?'

'Our canaries are still okay. I tell you, this whole G-M nerve gas thing is a put-on.'

'Then let's keep going.'

They sat in silence for a moment. Then both of them found handkerchiefs and tied them across the lower halves of their faces. Neary put the car in motion and they continued at a more prudent speed now that they were getting closer to the base of Devil's Tower.

He braked hard around a sharp bend, then had to stand on the pedal. Four olive-drab vans stood in a row, blocking the gravel trail. Neary shifted into reverse and craned his neck around to look out the rear window. As he started to back up, four more vans pulled in behind him.

'Uh-oh.'

Jillian and Neary rolled up their windows and locked the car doors without consulting each other. For a moment, nothing happened. Then the van doors opened and figures started coming out into the open sunlight. They looked like golden people.

It was impossible to tell whether they were military or not, but they were all dressed alike in sealed astronaut-type one-piece golden plastic suits with Plexiglas bubble helmets and tanks strapped to their backs. They seemed to be hermetically sealed inside by the shiny, metallic plastic. Neary thought they looked like a cooking-foil commercial.

One of them advanced cautiously until he was standing in front of the Vega. He then held up a small blackboard on which a message had been chalked:

'HOW DO YOU FEEL?'

The inanity of the question broke Neary's tension. He rolled down the window on his side. 'Fine!' he yelled. 'How do you clowns feel?'

The man in the gold suit put away the blackboard and gestured to them to get out of the car.

'The hell with that,' Neary snapped. 'The only gas in this area is from you guys farting around.'

Another golden man with a Red Cross insignia on his right arm, reached in and took the birdcage out of Jillian's hand. He walked to the front of the Vega and held it up for Neary to see. Both birds were lying on their backs, motionless.

177

Neary surrendered.

As soon as he and Jillian got out of the Vega, each was given a face mask and taken to a different van. 'Hey!' Neary yelled as the van with Jillian moved off. But his followed an instant later.

Inside, the vans had been equipped as mobile medical centres. The men in the golden suits, Neary supposed, were in fact some sort of medics. It seemed to him, however, that they were functioning more as guards than doctors. He had no way of looking outside as the van jolted along rough terrain for some time.

When at last the trip was over and the medic-guard opened the van's rear door, Neary saw that the sun was starting to set. Its horizontal rays slanted sideways through a small campground of trailer-offices, green tents and vans like the one in which he'd been brought here.

In the distance, hard to make out in the spreading darkness, technicians were busy unloading the trailers of a great number of heavy semi-rigs. No time to witness more.

A golden medic helped him into one of the sealed coffin-sized trailers. Since the man was still wearing his bubble, he said nothing, nor did Neary. Time passed. Neary glanced at his watch. Seven p.m.

Suddenly the trailer doors swung open. Two masked men came in through the airlock. The man in the golden plastic suit immediately left. Neary had been sitting on the edge of an examining table. He stared at the tall, thin, grey-haired man, then at the younger man beside him as they removed their face masks.

'Well?' he asked. 'You the honcho?'

The white-haired man frowned and turned to the other. *'Comment? Qu'est-ce que c'est un "honcho"?*

The other man grinned. *'Le grand fromage,'* he responded. He turned back to Neary.

'We have very little time, Mr. Neary,' he snapped. 'This is Mr. Lacombe. We need answers from you that are expressly honest, direct, and to the point.'

'So do I,' Neary countered. 'Where's Jillian?'

'Your friend is in no danger,' Laughlin said.

Lacombe sat down across from Neary. His blue-green eyes seemed to crackle slightly with . . . Neary couldn't be sure . . . annoyance, amazement? Lacombe delivered a barrage of French with Laughlin translating merely syllables behind him. 'Are you aware,' he said, 'of the danger you and your companion risked?'

Neary was confused by the French and the English. Who should he speak to, the man with the authority or the man who was speaking English. 'What danger?'

'There are toxins in the area,' the two men told him.

'We're alive. I'm alive. I'm talking.'

Laughlin continued translating rapidly. 'If the wind had shifted to the south, we would not be having this conversation.'

'There's nothing wrong with the air,' Neary insisted doggedly.

The Frenchman ran his fingers through unruly grey hair. He pulled a pencil from inside his jacket and propped up a clipboard on the edge of a desk.

'Some questions, Mr. Neary. Do you have any objections?'

'What kind of questions?'

Lacombe scanned the xeroxed sheet. Laughlin translated. 'For example: do you suffer from insomnia?'

'No.'

'Headaches?'

'No.'

'Have you ever been treated for a mental illness?'

'Not yet.' Neary's weak laugh produced no response. 'No.'

'Anyone in your family so treated?'

'No.'

Lacombe's pencil raced down the sheet of paper, making marks. 'Bad dreams?'

'No.'

'Have you recently had a skin disorder?'

'No. Not unless—'

'Yes?' the Frenchman prompted.

'Sort of a one-sided sunburn. But I wasn't out in the sun.'

The piercing blue-green eyes stared thoughtfully at him for a moment. Laughlin translated. 'About the bad dreams. Do you wish to reconsider your answer?'

'No. Well...' Neary paused. 'I had this *thing*. This, uh, thing in mind.'

Lacombe waited, pencil poised. 'More specific, please.'

Neary shrugged. 'It wasn't really much ... Just an idea.'

The Frenchman frowned and checked his wristwatch. He ran his pencil down the list and picked up the next question. 'Have you ever heard voices?'

'No voices. No little green men.'

'Mr. Neary,' Lacombe began carefully, slowly. 'Have you ever had a close encounter? A close encounter with something very unusual?'

That one clicked and Neary started a sloppy smile, 'Who are you guys?' He searched them for a few specific truths. He was on the street and they had his candy. But this wasn't fair play, only one piece at a time.

Lacombe looked up and offered another piece. 'Ever hear a ringing in the ears?' Laughlin interpreted. 'An almost agreeable, sometimes pleasant ringing? A particularly melodic tone or series of tones?'

'Who are you people?' Neary insisted.

Lacombe spoke in whispers to Laughlin. They were exchanging notes in French and Neary just sat there on his stool, feeling complete isolation.

'Is that it?' Neary cried. 'Is that all you're going to ask me?' The frustration of these absurd weeks surged out of him. 'Well . . . I got a couple of thousand goddamn questions! Are you the head man around here? I want to lodge a complaint. You have no right to make people crazy! You think I personally investigate every news story on Walter Cronkite? If this is just a cloud of gas . . . why is it I know this mountain in every detail, and I've never been here?'

Neary had spoken the magic words and now it was Lacombe who 'clicked'.

The Frenchman stopped and studied this strange American. There was a knock on the door. Bad timing. Another golden man – without medical insignia – stepped inside.

'Com-Sec says take them to Evac-Reliance and a bus ride home' one of the bubble-headed fellows said.

The character backed out of the room.

Lacombe returned to his seat and motioned to Neary and Laughlin to do the same. Now Lacombe was quite excited. 'You tell me,' he said in slow, careful English, 'you imagined this mountain before you had discovered its existence? It manifested itself to you in many ways. Shadows on the wall, ideas, geometric images that to you, Mr. Neary, seemed like progress toward the familiar but sadly and for so long without any meaning until, finally, it came to you. And it was right!!'

Neary held back his tears with great effort. He nodded bleakly.

'And you feel ...' Lacombe paused, obviously searching for just the right word. He found it. '*Compelled* to be here?'

'I guess you might say that,' Roy responded out of the depths of an irony he had never known he possessed.

Ignoring that, Lacombe took an envelope from David Laughlin, opened it and produced a dozen coloured Polaroids which he handed to Neary.

'These people? These are all people who were trying to get to the mountain. They are strangers to you?'

Roy went through the stack. 'Yes,' he said. 'All except her.' He held up Jillian's picture.

Lacombe took all the pictures back, put them in the envelope and gave it back to Laughlin.

'By being here,' the Frenchman asked quietly, 'what do you expect to find?'

Neary struggled to formulate a reply. What the hell *was* he doing here? 'The answer,' he said, at last. 'That's not crazy, is it?'

Lacombe got up to go. 'No, Mr. Neary, it is not.' When he reached the door he turned back quickly, spoke simply, 'I want to say to you that you are not alone. I wish you could know this. You have many friends and . . . I envy you.'

The three men passed in the airlock to put their helmets on. On a long wall table lay five or six unused masks, some long rubber gloves and a cheap birdcage. In it were two canaries. They huddled together in a corner and watched Neary's movements with too-bright eyes. Laughlin opened the outer door of the airlock and the three men walked into the early evening.

The sky in the west still glowed red, but overhead the heavens had darkened to a deep velvety blue. Neary glanced up and saw stars coming out in clusters through the thin mountain air.

Lacombe and his interpreter walked him to a Huey assault chopper, its engines purring but its rotor still.

'No!' Neary exclaimed. 'I'm not going back. I'm not going on any bus ride home!'

A gloved hand slid open the starboard door. Neary could see seven or eight civilians, all wearing masks, seated inside. Jillian lifted her hand listlessly, as if she had no energy left. Neary climbed aboard. One of the copter pilots handed a packet to Laughlin, standing on the ground below.

Laughlin leafed through the packet of paper and

cardboard. He passed it along to Lacombe. 'You see? Everyone drew his own version of the Tower before they came here.'

The Frenchman studied the drawings, some no more than doodles, some carefully done in crayon or felt-tipped pen. After a long moment he looked up through the open door of the Huey and stared at the people inside. Then his sharp glance shifted to the pilot and he spoke quickly to Laughlin in French.

'You are not to take off,' Laughlin relayed to the pilot.

'Sir, I have my orders from Com-Sec.'

'You have my orders now. No departure.'

'Sorry, sir,' the pilot said in a mulish tone. There was something about the 'sorry' that conveyed its opposite and something about the 'sir' that downgraded it to an epithet.

'Five minutes, then!' Lacombe snapped.

The pilot relented and held up three fingers.

Lacombe and Laughlin were off and running toward an O.D. trailer a hundred yards closer to the Devil's Tower.

TWENTY-THREE

The communications trailer was darkened at one end to allow the radar specialists to watch their scopes. At the other end, where a window looked out at the waiting helicopter in the distance, two civilians – Lacombe and Laughlin – were squared off with the Project Security Officer, a major known to them as Wild Bill, although the name tag on his chest indicated a less-colourful 'Walsh.'

Wild Bill was about Lacombe's age, forty-five, David Laughlin estimated, but that was the only similarity between the two men. Wild Bill was short, squat and loud. He had a flat, monotonous drawl, as if face-to-face conversation between humans was of the same order of verbal traffic as between control tower and passing aircraft, or between NASA Mission Control and an orbiting satellite crew.

'You cannot send them away,' the Frenchman burst out, more agitated than his interpreter had ever seen him. 'I will be responsible.'

'Half a minute, sir!' Wild Bill drawled, holding up one beefy hand, like a traffic cop. 'You have no responsibility this side of Mayflower. This is Security's operation.'

Lacombe began pacing about the end of the trailer as if caged. He was full of important new information and he wanted to be clearly understood in Wild Bill's language, not his own. David Laughlin decided that he had to try to help his boss, in his own words, for once.

'You don't understand,' Laughlin said, trying to break up the irreversible conflict shaping between the two men. 'Whatever you're doing down here at the base camp is for only one reason, so Mr. Lacombe's project can proceed on schedule upstairs.'

'I appreciate that.' Wild Bill's eyes, each neatly imbedded in a tight half-moon of suety flesh, almost closed shut as he grimaced. 'But you people have to understand how military discipline works.'

'I don't want those people removed,' the Frenchman repeated.

Wild Bill took a long, steadying breath. 'We have a chain of command three weeks long,' the major went on. 'This incursion into base camp . . . How do we know these aren't saboteurs, fanatics or cultists on a negative errand. That's the only way our chain of command is set up to handle an incursion. It's too late to handle it any other way.'

'This is a small group of people,' Lacombe said, speaking very slowly and turning now and then for a helping word from Laughlin, who was magnificent, supplying the emotional and linguistic word equivalents when Lacombe's excitement forced him to shift to his native tongue. He gestured out the window at the waiting helicopter. 'They share a common vision. It is a mystery to them and to me why they felt compelled to come here.'

Wild Bill hunched his meaty shoulders in a bull-like shrug. 'You want to go over my head for clearance, you'll have to copter out the message because we've got communications blacked out down here to the point where even I don't know what's going on.'

The Frenchman shoved a handful of drawings at the major. 'Why were these not shown to me until the last moment?'

Wild Bill took the bits of paper and spread them out on the table: 'Interesting,' he mused.

'We know very little about these people,' Lacombe told him. 'Just the answers to our questionnaire. But *who* are they? *Why* did they all draw these pictures? *Why* were they compelled to come here when they saw Devil's Tower on television?'

The tubby man shrugged. 'Got to be coincidence.' Obviously unhappy with the idea, he continued pushing around the drawings with one pudgy finger. 'These are just a random assortment of people,' he said then. 'Nothing special about them. This guy Neary you talked to. He's Mr. Joe Blow. The woman with him says she's looking for her little boy. Who knows?'

'What about this one?' Lacombe demanded, pointing to a larger drawing in some detail. The major turned it over and read the name of the artist on the back. 'Larry Fownen. We checked him out. He's from Los Angeles. Sells real estate. Used to be a bit player in Western flicks. He's another nobody.'

'This one?' the Frenchman wanted to know.

Wild Bill stared at the scrawled crayon sketch. 'A Mrs. Rosen from Kansas City. She's a grandmother. Her husband is with her. Retired. On vacation. We ran checks on all these people, direct to Washington. They're nobodies. A few traffic violations. No criminal records.'

'And this one?'

'George Fender. Garage mechanic, Forth Worth,

Texas. World War II veteran. Wounded on Guadal-canal.'

'This one?'

'We don't have this kind of time,' the major said. 'Take my word for it. These folks are nothing.'

'This one?' Lacombe insisted.

'Elaine Connelly. School teacher. Bethesda, Mary-land. Widow. Married son, three grandchildren.' Wild Bill gave a snort of exasperation. 'I suppose you want a rundown on the other two?'

'Of course!' Lacombe responded.

'Mr. & Mrs. Arthur Penderecki, Hampramck, Michigan. He's a meat cutter. She's a secretary. They're on their honeymoon. She teaches Sunday School.' He took a sharp breath. 'Enough!' he snapped then.

'But there is no connection,' the Frenchman said.

'I don't care whether there is or there isn't. My responsibility is to ship the lot of them off the premises. Now!'

'But you have said it yourself. They are not harmful people. They are nobody in particular.'

'That's how they *seem*,' the major reminded him. 'On a quick five-minute check, that's all we've uncovered.'

'Nine people who had the same vision.'

'So they say.'

'Who have the same compulsion to come here.'

'We're wasting time,' Wild Bill said in a controlled yelp. 'It's not my time. It's your time. You're the man with the deadline. But once you make it my deadline, that's it. We move. Now!'

Lacombe said nothing for a long moment. His grey-haired head had reared back on his neck during this confrontation. Now it relaxed slightly. 'I must find out what is the meaning of these people's compulsion. Why they had to come here. Maybe—'

'No way,' Wild Bill snapped.

'*Écoutez-moi!*' Lacombe snarled angrily. 'For every one of these people there must be thousands out there also touched by this implanted vision.'

'It's just a coincidence,' the major suggested.

'It is a sociological event,' the Frenchman corrected him, 'of surprising importance. The answer to why they've come is perhaps the most important information we will have developed in the Project's entire existence.'

'I'm terminating this conversation.'

Lacombe's arm reached out. His fingers grabbed the front of Wild Bill's combat jacket. 'You will listen to me, major Walsh.'

Wild Bill's tiny eyes widened. Nobody had grabbed the front of his jacket since he'd been a lieutenant fresh from the Point.

'You're gonna be late upstairs at the D.S.M.' he told the Frenchman.

'*Écoutez-moi, tête-de-merde.*'

Wild Bill turned to Laughlin. 'Wha'd he say?'

189

TWENTY-FOUR

Inside the big Huey helicopter, Neary, Jillian and the other civilians who had 'incursed' the base camp sat quietly, almost numbly, gas masks fastened, only their eyes moving this way and that as they tried to understand what had happened to them.

What was going to happen now, Neary told himself, was obvious. They'd be lifted out in another few minutes and that would be the end of the whole wild thing. He'd never learn what the mountain meant. Jillian would never find Barry. None of these people would ever know anything.

And all because the base camp's strategy for keeping out visitors was hard to beat. The advertised nerve gas danger could be real. It would be like the military, he mused, to actually let a few whiffs of it into the area and knock off enough wildlife to convince the skeptics, or were the wildlife only stunned? Neary remembered the two canaries in the cheap metal cage sitting inside the air lock of one of the trailers. Whose canaries? His? But he'd been shown his canaries were dead. If not dead. . . .

He was sitting next to Jillian, their thighs pressed against each other, her eyes closed. She'd come a long, long way, Neary thought, and for nothing. They had all killed themselves to get here. And now it was going to be over before it even began.

He got to his feet. The seven other civilians

glanced at him. Jillian's eyes opened and she looked up at him.

Slowly, moving with great precision, Neary unfastened his gas mask. The snaps made noises like rifle shots. He ripped off the mask and threw it to the ground. If this was the bravest thing he'd ever done, it was also, all of a sudden, the easiest. It made the most sense, too.

He took in a long deep breath.

The others looked horrified. Then, so fast he almost missed the movement, Jillian tore the mask from her face. She stood up beside Neary and took a full breath.

'You'll be poisoned,' a little 70-year-old man told him.

'Mister,' Neary told him, 'there is nothing wrong with this air. The military just doesn't want any witnesses here.'

A little old lady, perhaps the little old man's wife, said quiveringly, 'But if the Army doesn't want us here, this isn't our business.'

'We only wanted to see the mountain,' the old man said apologetically to Neary. 'It was such a coincidence when I painted it. No one bothered to tell us about the air.'

'How did you locate this spot?' Jillian asked him.

'No problem. I looked it up in *Famous Mountains of the Western Hemisphere*. Did you know that President Theodore Roosevelt proclaimed this our country's first national monument on September 24, 1906?'

A fellow in his forties stood up and ripped off his helmet. He had a suntan, longish hair and acted like a guy with a lot of money. He took a deep breath, exhaled and then said, 'Oh, Christ! It's better than the air in Los Angeles.'

Two others – a man and a woman – stood up and with nervous, trembling fingers, took off their helmets. Their faces were drawn and thin, and they had the look of people on the downside of physical exhaustion, people who had probably been socially criticised for months. They looked scooped out from the inside, and they were unable to make eye contact with Neary or the others.

Roy turned to face all his companions. He spoke loudly above the idling rotors. 'Who's for staying?' he asked.

Jillian raised her hand. Then the fellow from Los Angeles. Finally, the old couple. Everyone else looked away.

'O.K.,' Neary said. 'You'll have to keep up with me and run very fast.'

At that moment, the helicopter door started sliding shut behind him. Roy desperately used his arm as a door jam. The guard outside opened the door to see what was going on and saw a bunch of the detainees with their helmets off. As he was registering this, the fellow from Los Angeles rushed to Neary's side.

'Now!' Roy shouted. *'Run for the mountain!'*

They pushed the door halfway open and Neary struck out and hit the guard in the neck, just under his helmet, with his foot. Roy, Jillian and the Los Angeles man vaulted awkwardly over the fallen soldier and headed for the tree line.

Piggly-Wiggly and Baskin Robbins trucks where technicians – without helmets and space suits – were unloading electronic equipment and a lot of crates labeled Lockheed and Rockwell – Special Handling flashed by their eyes as they darted away.

The other detainees, including the old couple, who decided to run for it were stopped by the other guards within two steps of the helicopter door. Neary was running with every fibre of strength and glanced up at the mountain that had haunted their dreams. Now they would get the chance to unravel the nightmare.

Back in the communications trailer, Lacombe, utterly frustrated by Wild Bill's ignorance and intransigence, said in failing English, 'You do not understand!' Then, in rapid-fire French: 'The mountain was the key. And the gift in the Mexican desert was a clue. For us, to open our minds and let them in.'

Laughlin finished translating, and then Lacombe had a new thought. He translated it himself from the French. *'They were invited!'* he shouted. *'They were invited!'*

None of this sank in. Laughlin could see that.

But something outside the window caught Lacombe's eye. He drifted over and watched the three detainees heading for the trees. He didn't say anything, but a slow smile spread over his face.

Meanwhile, Wild Bill was letting loose a blast at David Laughlin. 'You have a job I am told is among the high rungs around here. My work isn't so lofty but without the services we perform you'd miss a step and fall through. There are no star pitchers in this bullpen, no boss cows . . .'

Lacombe got the drift of it and then stopped listening. He watched the three escapees disappear into the trees with great satisfaction.

After they were gone, he turned back to Laughlin, still smiling, and said, 'Translate.'

David had completely blown his cool, listening to this asshole. He turned to Lacombe and said, in French, 'A lot of shit!'

'I thought so,' said the Frenchman, still smiling some more.

Moving in the shadows of dusk, Neary led his two companions around a helicopter pad and into the brushlands at the base of the mountain. He fell to the ground to catch his breath and to give the others a chance to catch up with him. When they did, Roy started taking off his space suit and motioned to them to do the same.

He stuck out his ungloved hand. 'Hiya. Name's Roy.'

'Larry Butler.'

Still puffing hard, Neary said, 'We can't stay here. Go on to the tree line and wait for me there.'

Larry and Jillian took off immediately. Roy took another moment to catch his breath, looking down at the activities at the base camp and then he, too, started running hard up the mountain toward the tree line, two hundred yards away.

A moaning siren howled in the darkness. Search-lights began to crisscross the landing pad. The door to the communications trailer burst open, and a guard, gasping for breath inside his helmet, stumbled in.

'Overpowered me, sir!'

'How many?' Wild Bill barked.

'Three. Three of them, sir. We got the rest.'

Wild Bill grabbed a pair of binoculars off the table, glanced darkly at Lacombe and Laughlin and strode fast out of the trailer. The others followed.

In the background, three helicopters were already rising vertically, testing their powerful Quartz-Iodide searchlights. About a dozen Special Forces soldiers in regular gear, including gas masks strapped to their belts, were loading their rifles. They were carrying semi-automatic M-14s with infrared sniper sights.

Wild Bill swept the tree line with his binoculars. They had set up an improvised field headquarters near the helicopter pads. The major and Lacombe were on two field phones.

'I'll have them off the mountain in one hour,' Wild Bill shouted into his phone.

A voice responded on their phones. 'Do a photometric analysis of the northern face. Use infrared.'

'It's already ordered.'

'If they are not off the mountain by 0800 hours, dust the northern face with E-Z Four. Get back to me.'

'What is . . . E-Z Four?' Lacombe asked, alarmed.

'A sleep aerosol,' Wild Bill told him on the telephone, although they were standing two feet apart. 'Same stuff we've been using on the livestock decoys. It's fast-acting, extremely local, and should detoxify in several hours. They'll be out cold for six hours and looking for coffee by sunup.'

In careful English, the Frenchman spoke into his phone. 'We do not choose this place. We do not choose this time. We do not choose these people. To stop them is not for us to choose.'

'This was a perfect strategic vacuum until he siphoned air into it,' Wild Bill told the phone.

'They belong here more than we,' Lacombe said sadly.

Through the fir trees the top of Devil's Tower stood out against the evening sky. It appeared insurmountable to the three escapees as they trudged wearily up a steep incline, slipping in the loose topsoil and pine needles.

Jillian stumbled and fell, sliding backwards, downwards before catching hold of some undergrowth. Larry Butler also fell, but was up in a moment. Roy stopped, waiting for them to catch up to him. Then he heard the by-now-familiar noise above him.

Suddenly three helicopters lit up the uppermost region of the mountain top way ahead of them and started manoeuvring around the partially-hidden areas, poking away at them with their brilliant searchlights.

'They've given us a lot of credit,' Larry said, breathing heavily. 'That's a good two hours on foot.'

'Do you see that notch in the mountain?' Neary asked, pointing through the darkness.

There was, in fact, a narrow passage through to the other side.

'We can probably make that in no time,' he said, trying to cheer himself up, as well as Jillian and Larry.

Butler got set to make the dash. 'I should've never given up jogging,' he said, grinning.

A formation of red and green helicopter lights

hovered above the plateau and then disappeared as the choppers started to sweep the far side of the mountain.

'There go four more,' Jillian counted. 'There's another ravine that leads up the hill,' she said hesitantly. 'I remember it from my painting... It's an easier climb. It starts on the northeast face and—'

'That's no good,' Neary said definitively. 'It falls off at the top three hundred feet straight down. We'd have to be experienced climbers. This way, it's a gradual roll to the other side.'

'What do you think is on the other side?' Butler asked.

'There's a box canyon. It's rimmed with trees and hiking trails.'

Jillian looked at Neary. 'I never imagined that,' she said. 'I just coloured the one side.'

'There was no canyon in my doodles,' Larry agreed.

'Next time,' Neary said, breaking into a short laugh, 'try sculpture.'

Back at the bivouac area, near the helicopter pad, a group of Army engineers were relaying ten gallon stainless steel canisters of E-Z Four to the waiting helicopters. The men worked in silence beneath the howling rotors and handled the stuff as though it might spill out at any moment and fell them all.

Wild Bill stood off to the side, watching the operation. He checked his watch and looked up the mountain. He knew the platoon of Special Forces troops had fanned out and were moving steadily up the mountain, pausing from time to time to sweep the forest with the special infrared scopes mounted on their M-14s.

An aide handed Wild Bill a field phone.

'Pyramid to Bahama.'

'Bahama,' Wild Bill answered. 'Go 'head.'

'Nothing to report from mid-station. Once they reach the shoulder there's a thousand places for concealment. I'd need three times the ground force to cover this whole mountain in one hour.'

Wild Bill held the phone away from his ear, cogitating. Then he spoke quickly into it. 'Return to base-line.'

The major handed the instrument back to an aide, thought for another moment, and said, 'Get everybody off the northern face. Call the dark side of the moon and tell them we're going to dust.'

Lacombe emerged from the communications trailer and was holding a sports jacket on a cellophane-covered wire hanger. He walked across the pad toward a waiting transport helicopter, Laughlin trailing him. The Frenchman stopped to watch Wild Bill give the order to the E-Z-Four-loaded helicopters. They revved up to a screaming level then, one at a time, the three choppers lifted off vertically and then in follow-the leader style headed up and off into the night, their red and green lights blinking.

The Frenchman gazed hard at Wild Bill, more in sorrow than in anger. Then he followed Laughlin and five button-down civilian operators onto the Huey. The door was immediately slid shut and in a second the big cargo helicopter also rose vertically and headed off into the night.

On the mountain, Roy, Jillian and Larry were on the far side of exhaustion. They had worked their way nearly around to the back side of the mountain. From what Neary remembered of the model he had made, the box canyon couldn't be too far away. And he'd been right about the helicopters. They weren't dusting this section. So far.

A clearing lay ahead.

'Let's make a run for it,' he said to Jillian and Larry.

Jillian simply nodded, saving her breath, but Larry, who was really shot, gasped, 'Go ahead. I'll catch up.'

'All right,' Roy said. 'We'll wait for you on the other side.'

He took off running, crouched low to the ground, Jillian right behind him. In less than a minute, they had made it across the open space and thrown themselves down on the pine needles, panting and gasping. They were very thirsty, dripping with perspiration, and their hands and faces stung from numberless bramble and branch slaps. Somewhere along the line, perhaps in the helicopter door, Neary had damaged his left arm and shoulder. When he stopped to think about it, he was in considerable pain, and he was starting to lose the use of the arm.

They lay on their stomachs, looking for Larry.

'There!' Jillian whispered, pointing to the left.

They watched Butler emerge from the tree cover a good hundred yards downwind of them.

'Larry!' Roy called. 'Over here!'

A perfectly terrible explosion of noise and light overwhelmed his call as an assault chopper trimmed the tree tops, its powerful belly-light sweeping across the clearing.

Roy and Jillian stood up now, waving Larry toward them. The noise grew louder, but Neary shouted anyway, 'You're in the clear . . . he'll spot you.'

The helicopter swooped over, making a sharp bank above them. It must have seen the man in the clearing.

Larry had heard both the chopper and Neary, because he shouted up to them, using valuable lung power, 'Screw 'em . . . So what's he gonna do? Land on me?'

The helicopter came down over them and then headed for the clearing down below. Small birds started dropping out of tree tops off to the side. Neary and Jillian realised that they had to get upwind of the stuff. And fast. They were only fifty yards from the notch. Too exhausted to do anything more, they began crawling.

Behind them, the helicopter hovered, screaming, right over Larry. He seemed totally unconcerned in the middle of the noise, the little cyclone of needles, brush and leaves, and the invisible E-Z Four. He stuck up his thumb, like a hitchhiker, and yelled, 'Look, they're only cropdusting!'

By the time Roy and Jillian had painfully crawled their way to the summit of the notch and looked back down, Larry Butler, still walking, was starting to twitch spasmodically. First his head, then his arms. He started to stagger.

Jillian started to get up. She was going to run

down to him. Neary grabbed her. 'No, no!' he shouted in her ear. 'Don't look down.' Jillian sank back.

They watched Larry fall, try to get up, twitch horribly on the open ground and then lie still.

They stood there, gazing out into the clearing. The tall grass was down in one place where Larry's body lay. 'We shouldn't just leave him out there,' Jillian said at last.

'If he's sleeping, he can do it there as well as here.'

'And if he's dying' Jillian asked.

'If he's dying . . .' Neary took another breath, then expelled it with a puffing sound . . . 'then so are we'.

Jillian's arm gave him a squeeze.

They moved off through the tall pines, heading toward the ridge. The way Neary remembered it, sculptured in mud and newspaper and chicken wire, the ridge provided a kind of gallery that ran around the canyon, a place shrouded by trees.

Even before they reached the ridge, a strong light seemed to be coming from just below it, a steady glow reflecting back in the dark night from tiny droplets of water vapour in the high, clear air. As they neared the edge, they dropped to their bellies and snaked forward for a cautious peek.

It was an uphill crawl along a thirty-foot stretch of slope. Neary could hear the helicopter coming back around the mountain. He reached for a scrawny bush to get a handhold, missed.

He slid back down the slope. 'Roy!' Jillian called from her position at the top of the ridge. 'Come on, Roy! You can make it!'

He was sweating. His legs ached. His fingers

couldn't seem to grip. 'Please, Roy! The helicopter's coming.'

Neary squinted up at her. Jillian was reaching down the slope for his hand. He began to crawl. The agony of it took his breath away. Inches at a move through loose-packed, sandy dirt. Inches.

'Roy, just a few feet more.'

The chopper's *rat-a-tat* was louder. Sweat poured down Neary's forehead and into his eyes. He was only a yard from Jillian's outstretched hand. Half a yard.

The beat of the rotors filled the air overhead. At any moment the hissing sound of gas would come. Neary's whole body buckled convulsively. He threw himself forward. Jillian caught his hand.

She helped pull him up over the rim of the slope. They tumbled head over heels down a reverse incline and came to rest at the very rim of the canyon below.

The helicopter yammered past. Neary stared up at it through sweat-smeared eyes. No spray. They were too close to the canyon. They were safe.

He let out a great, shuddering sigh and took in a big lungful of fresh air. Then he and Jillian moved forward to stare over the brink of the canyon. Together they reached the edge of the outcropped plateau and peered over. Below was a sight they could not absorb.

'Christ!' Neary breathed.

'Oh, God!' Jillian cried. 'Oh, my God!'

TWENTY-FIVE

Nature had ended and Man had taken over.

It looked like a sky harbour, a sort of cosmic port of call, manufactured by humans. There were landing lights stretching out to the horizon, perhaps five miles away, Neary estimated. Right in the centre of the whole incredible base, the runway lights led up to a huge lighted double cross that was ringed by small strobe lights. It looked to Neary like a place where something was supposed to set down.

The entire area, which had been dynamited and bulldozed flat, was ringed by big stadium lights perched on metal standards. Under the brilliant lights, Roy and Jillian could see that the whole base was circumscribed by a six-foot-high steel retaining wall. Inside there were three levels and on each level there were many self-contained modular cubicles, all with two doors, some with big picture windows and some without windows. The cubicles were of different sizes and heights, perched on metal scaffolds and reached by ladders.

Upfield and in the centre of the huge arena was a colour-sound scoreboard that must have been forty feet long and six feet high, standing on a sixteen-foot scaffold and connected by many cables and conduits to a big Moog synthesizer on the ground downfield.

Without turning, Neary said, 'Do you see that?'

'Oh, yes!' Jillian whispered.

'Good,' Roy said, relieved to have received confirmation that he was not hallucinating or at least that he was not hallucinating alone.

They were two hundred, perhaps three hundred feet above the great open-ended stadium that had been blasted and carved out of the box canyon, and as their eyes and minds adjusted to the fantastic scene below, Roy and Jillian, without saying anything more, decided to scramble down lower and closer. They moved cautiously down the granite edges to a perch some fifty feet below where the brush provided excellent cover.

Now they could make out men, technicians apparently, working in and around the cubicles. They were dressed in jumpsuits – the white ones had 'McDonnell-Douglas' written on the backs, the blue, 'Rockwell,' and the red 'Lockheed.' The cubicles seemed to be set up as small laboratories. Roy and Jill could not make out what all the equipment was for, but they did recognise some laser apparatus, bio-chemical instruments, devices for thermal and electromagnetic measurements, looking like bazookas on their tripods, a couple of spectographic analyzers, and a lot of complicated-looking instruments intended to monitor and measure God only knew what.

Inside three of the cubicles sat black-suited men, all wearing dark glasses, obviously VIPs, guarded by military personnel, the only military that Neary could spot. Around the base were great radar dishes, constantly panning around and occasionally stopping for a moment and then moving on again. There were television monitors everywhere and at least one hundred film cameras, fifty still cameras and twenty-five videotape TV cameras set in banks on swivels. There were perhaps thirty operators and loaders for all cameras, the rest evidently were operated by remote control and connected to the tracking radar.

Despite its size, the area was both cluttered and a mess. There were Coca-Cola and snack food machines scattered about indiscriminately, portable outhouses around the perimeter and a small catering area that resembled, to Roy, an Army soup kitchen under a canvas overhang. There were a lot of unopened crates that had McDonnell-Douglas, Rockwell and Lockheed markings on the sides, and there was debris – paper cups, napkins, plates, toilet paper, empty soda cans everywhere. In fact, some guys in jumpsuits were sweeping up the stuff just as an apparent tour of executives in sunglasses, led by a white-haired man in a jumpsuit, strolled by.

A bunch of technicians were clustered around the synthesizer and one character, at the urging of the others, sat down at the large console and began picking out 'Moon River' with one finger. The squeals and wows echoed across the canyon and vague forms of light and colour shifted and faded across the giant scoreboard. The 'musician' was shouted down by other technicians across the gridiron.

'I know what this is!' Neary said, more to himself than to Jill. 'I know what this is! This is unbelievable!'

A gentle chime sounded below them.

'Gentlemen, ladies . . .'

A voice came over the loudspeaker system. He must have been in one of the cubicles, perhaps the communications cubicle, the one with all the computers. No, now they saw him.

A fellow in a white jumpsuit, holding a small microphone, the cord trailing out behind him, was walking out to the centre of the arena. 'Gentlemen, ladies. Take your positions, please. This is not a drill. I repeat: this is not a drill. Could we have the lights in the arena down to 60 degrees? Please. Sixty degrees on the lights.'

Gradually the stadium lights started dimming, and the landing lights were dialled up. For five miles down the strip – all the way to the horizon – Roy and Jillian watched the lights come up. Suddenly they noticed that inside the modules the computer and instrument lights were going from white to red. Red working lights were now glowing from almost all the cubicles.

'Good, good, good,' the man who was acting like a master of ceremonies enthused. 'I don't think we could ask for a more beautiful evening. Do you? . . . Well, if everyone is ready . . .'

Neary understood that these several hundred scientists and technicians had been holding a vigil every night for some time, and every night had been a false alarm. Nothing had happened. No one had come. Now he noticed that all the radar dishes had stopped sweeping and were focused in one direction, directly at them.

'They're staring at us,' Jillian gasped, scrunching down even flatter on the rock.

'Not at us. At the sky. Look.'

Roy and Jill turned their faces to the stars.

Something was beginning.

At first, Neary and Jillian had no idea what it was. Their eyes slowly adjusted from the glare of the stadium lights to the almost total darkness above them. The first thing they picked out was the Milky Way, then in the northern sky they saw the constellation of Orion. They stared hard at the cluster of stars they had seen so often before.

They were moving. The stars were moving.

The stars that made up the constellation shifted slowly at first, then more rapidly, some edging away, leaving the constellation.

Neary turned to search the sky. He found another Orion at the opposite horizon.

'There's the real one,' he said, pointing it out to Jillian.

When they looked back at the changing Orion, it had already become something different, its 'stars', which clearly were not stars, shifting constantly. A number of them had moved until they had formed an almost evenly-spaced curved line. Then from the end 'star,' as if attracted by it, three more moved in with majestic speed to form an oblong shape.

The Big Dipper.

Neary started laughing. He was no longer afraid at all. He was just very happy.

Below them, the hundreds of scientists and technicians were reacting like ordinary mortals at a show of fireworks, 'oohhing' and 'aahhing' and finally bursting into applause when the Dipper was fully formed.

'We're the only ones who know. The only ones,' Roy said. 'Did you see that?' he asked her, checking.

'Yes,' Jillian reassured him and herself.

'Good.'

All of a sudden what appeared to be three shooting stars came out of the western sky. They shot right overhead and abruptly stopped, as if putting on brakes, in mid-space, exploding in a moment every known law of gravity and physics. The stars executed – on a dime – a complete 180-degree turn and then each point of light broke off into four different points and shot back off into the night sky.

Inside the stadium the audience went wild, as if reacting to their college marching band before the game.

Roy and Jill looked at each other.

'Did you see *that*?'

'Yes.'

'Good.'

The show was not over. It was, in fact, just beginning.

A cloud, what appeared to be a simple, lonely cloud, floated over the base, escorted by two very bright blue points of light within it. The two blue lights began to swirl faster and faster around the cloud, which started losing its form and then re-shaped itself into a design that resembled a spiral nebula.

One of the lights penetrated the nebula and turned on even more brightly so that the whole cloud was lit up from within. No longer blue, but a deep amber. And then the other light took up a position in the outer arm of the spiral and began blinking on and off.

It was an extraordinary sight, a vision that seemed to flash and swirl with meaning, if only they could apprehend it. It was a demonstration, there was no doubt of that. But a cosmic demonstration of what? Of the place in the cosmic galaxy where we live? Yes! Perhaps that was it. A scale model of our planet's location. Incredible!

Roy and Jillian did not speak. They were trying to catch their breaths, trying to assimilate these sights and perceptions. They were crouched on a small promontory. Behind them was nothing, just the night sky and distance. Suddenly, in that sky, were clouds moving on both sides behind them. And from the clouds a light – like heat lightning behind the clouds, except when the light flashed stroboscopically it did not go off. The flash stayed on.

Then the light got brighter still in one part of the cloud, and bursting out of the cloud came an intensely bright pencil point of orange light, followed by two more brilliant pencil points of orange light. In a moment, as the lights approached at unbelievable speed in a sort of wing formation, Neary and Jillian just had time to cover their faces as the vehicles made a slow, screaming pass right over their heads.

They were the same ones – the monster kleig light, the flashing, beautifully coloured sunset, the enormous jack-o'-lantern with its leering, phantom face – that had appeared so spectacularly to them on the Indiana summit so many nights ago.

As these enormous furnace lights – vehicles without wings or physics, brilliant, flashing, coloured lights that blew away one's security, the belief in your own existence and that of the 'real' world – passed over them, a huge displacement of air and heat blew dust everywhere. Their hair went in all directions, the static electricity made all the hair on Neary's arms and chest stand up on end.

Again they felt buffeted and seared by the heat. Again the very breath was sucked out of their lungs. They had just enough time to inhale as each of the three vehicles, wailing mournfully like a million banshees, swept over. The time the sounds they made were frightening. A thousand voices wailing sending chills up their backs right in the middle of the intense heat. Neary realized that the sounds were the noises of alien machinery, but this realization did not make him feel any more secure.

By the time Roy and Jill had cleared the dust and the tears from their eyes, the monstrous, flashing, brilliantly-coloured vehicles were swooping low over the stadium area, sending the scoreboard off into a riot of scuttling colours – and sending the scientists and technicians scuttling for cover. The cameras followed the objects on their swivels and the radar dishes panned all the way round.

The brilliant objects passed over the double cross landing area that was flashing landing coordinates to them, swooped several hundred yards further down the concrete strip where there was nobody around, abruptly stopped as if putting on brakes and then just . . . hovered.

They hovered in a sort of triangle formation, their brilliant, almost-impossible-to-look-at colours holding steady. The objects seemed to settle close to the tarmac, perhaps as close as five feet above it, then they would pop back up to about twenty-five feet. They seemed to be almost flirting with the ground, playing, tasting it, licking up some dirt and debris, but then popping up as if actually frightened.

Neary was bug-eyed. He wanted to climb down closer to it all but realized that Jillian was too freaked out to move.

Meanwhile, something that Roy realized had been planned and rehearsed and rehearsed a hundred, a thousand times for just this historical moment began to unfold. The synthesizer was surrounded and boarded by a group of technicians wearing headsets and pencil microphones that they plugged into the console. Trailing their twenty-foot cords, they gathered around with their clipboards and penlights in hand.

One man, obviously the team leader, said into the almost-reverent hush, 'Gentlemen, thirty years of planning and preparation has come down to the few of us at this time. Let's do our jobs.' He stopped speaking to turn and face each man individually. 'All right, men. Shall we begin?'

In the communications booth, a technician spoke into his pencil mike. 'TC stereo. Time and resistance ... Auto ready. Tone interpolation on interlock.'

Another technician said, 'ARP interlock now! Speed set at seven and a half. All positive functions standing by. Sunset!'

'Go.'

Lacombe and David Laughlin, clad in white jumpsuits, also stood by the console of the synthesizer. Sitting now before the double keyboard was a young man who resembled William Shakespeare. He was obviously very nervous, perspiring heavily, wiping his face and hands on a handkerchief, clearly aware of the tremendous responsibility that lay upon him, the months and years of research and work and hope that had all come down to the few notes he was now going to sound. He must get them right.

The master of ceremonies said softly to him, 'Okay. Start with the tone.'

Shakespeare played the first note.

The booth technician spoke into his pencil microphone. 'Tang ... go!'

An amber light appeared on the giant scoreboard, fading and disappearing as the note floated away across the canyon.

'Up a full tone,' M.C. ordered, and Shakespeare sounded the second note.

The scoreboard lit up a deep pink.

'Down a major third.'

A new note and a new colour. Purple, this time.

'Now drop an octave.'

The fourth note echoed and a beautiful deep blue played across the scoreboard.

'Cool blue ... Go,' the booth technician ordered.

'Up a perfect fifth,' the M.C. said.

The last note sounded and faded away. The scoreboard flashed a brilliant red and faded.

'Nothing. Nothing at all,' the team leader said.

The M.C. said to Shakespeare, 'Give me a tone.'

A note sounded, a colour flashed, and the five note, five colour sequence was repeated, according to the M.C.'s instructions.

In the booth, the technician ordered, '*Ray* to the second. *Me* to the third. *Do* the first. *Do* one-half one, *So* to the fifth.'

The notes and the colours faded away across the arena, and there was still no response from the three objects. They just hovered downfield, flashing and blinking inscrutably.

Lacombe stepped up to the console and said, *'Encore. Une fois*. Again. One more time.'

The five-note sequence sounded and echoed through the night and the five colours played and danced across the scoreboard.

'Speak to me, speak to me,' the team leader pleaded.

'Plus vite,' Lacombe commanded. *'Plus vite.'*

Shakespeare did as he was ordered. This time the notes and the colours cascaded around the arena.

High above on their ledge, Jillian Guiler hummed the five-note sequence through twice. 'I know that,' she told Neary. Oh, my God, she thought. It's Barry's song. Jill was almost in shock, tears in her eyes, but Roy didn't notice.

Below, Lacombe was saying, 'Faster, Jean Claude. Faster. *Plus vite*. Faster.' He started walking down the landing strip toward the hovering vehicles. *'Plus vite. Plus vite.'*

The sweat was really pouring off Shakespeare now, dripping onto the keys of the synthesizer. He was playing the notes very fast and loud now, and the scoreboard was zooming from amber to pink to purple to blue to red.

Lacombe walked up the strip to within one hundred and fifty yards of the hovering, non-responding vehicles. The booth technician dialled the synthesizer all the way up and the notes reverberated hugely off the walls of the canyon.

The Frenchman had become very impatient. *'Qu'est ce que ce passe?'* he asked the objects. *Allez, allez, allez. Allons y.* Let's go.' Lacombe was shouting over the Moog, making the five-note hand movements.

'Say hello,' the booth technician ordered. 'Fire at will.'

Lacombe waved his hands at the hovering vehicles and called to the musician, *'Plus vite, plus vite,'* then headed back toward the console.

Shakespeare was playing his brains out and the scoreboard was flashing through the colours of the spectrum from ultraviolet to infrared and everything in between.

All of a sudden the vehicles responded. Not in sounds but in colours. They began to repeat the colours on the scoreboard. Each object was repeating separately the colours flashing across the board. Shakespeare stopped playing. As the notes faded away across the canyon, there was utter silence. For a long moment, all they could hear was the wind blowing down the canyon.

Then Lacombe pointed to Shakespeare and said, 'Come on. Keep going, keep going.'

The team leader exhorted his man on. 'Kick that mule, boy!'

The musician/engineer began playing very, very quickly and the scoreboard and the three vehicles picked up the action, changing colours in the same variation in total synchrony. The men around him were all sweating profusely, too, concentrating fiercely as the objects flashed their colours. They were filled with joy. In fact, they were beyond joy. In a state that no humans had previously experienced or described. For this was the first contact, the first contact in recorded history.

And suddenly the three objects stopped responding. They just flew off. In three different directions. One shot straight up and disappeared, lights off, apparently, into a large cloud. The other two swooped over the edge of the canyon and out of sight.

The music stopped. The scoreboard went to black. Silence. The wind.

And then the arena went crazy. Everyone began applauding and screaming. It was just like Mission Control after the Eagle had landed. These restrained, laid-back scientists and technicians were jumping up and down, hugging each other, shaking hands, pounding each other on the backs. The stadium lights came back on full, and the men in their jumpsuits and civilian clothes started coming out of their cubicles. Everything, it seemed, was over.

The booth technicians came down and sought out Lacombe and the team leader.

'Beautiful,' he said. 'Beautiful.'

Lacombe spoke to David Laughlin in English. 'I am very happy tonight.'

The team leader shook all their hands, including Shakespeare's. 'Congratulations. Not Merle Haggard, but it was great!'

Above this scene of jubilation, on their rocky ledge, Roy was completely elated and Jillian in tears. 'I know that sound,' she kept on saying. 'I just know it. I've heard it, I know that sound.'

Below, in one of the radar communications cubicles, a number of the instruments started showing red. The huge radar scoops had stopped sweeping again and all were focussed on the mountain above Neary and Jillian. Something was happening in the sky beyond the mountain.

On the floor of the stadium, one of the technicians approached the Frenchman, saying, 'Mr. Lacombe,' and pointed up.

Lacombe and Laughlin walked away from the back-slappers, looking up at the sky.

'What is it?' David Laughlin asked. 'What's happening?'

'*Je ne sais pas.*'

Roy and Jill turned, looking back and up toward where the men below were now all looking and pointing. Then they saw it, too.

A number of large cumulus clouds had formed in the sky over the mountain. Within the clouds was an extraordinary display of flashing pyrotechnics – like the Fourth of July, only better. It seemed to be a bizarre electrical storm different from anything that they had seen before and frightening in its size and intensity.

Simultaneously, and without words, Neary and Jillian felt that they must get away from the lights, get closer down to the base and other humans. So together they started the perilous scramble down. Jillian was terrified. The flashing clouds suddenly reminded her of the awful day that Barry was taken. Soundlessly, she communicated her terror to Roy.

The clouds had come down very close to the top of the mountain. There seemed to be more of them now. Suddenly zooming out of the clouds, one of the brilliantly lighted objects swept down across the arena, stopping just where it had hovered before. It hovered again and then suddenly flashed all its lights. Red. Three times.

It was, evidently, a signal of some kind.

The largest part of the cloud formation flashed

red three times. Then it flashed white and blue three times.

There was a brief pause during which all the technicians looked at each other uneasily. What the hell next?

Then the invasion began.

Out of the clouds burst a formation of fifty pinpoints of light that swiftly materialized into flying objects of weird shapes and colours. And tricks. These crazy things were performing low level aerial tricks for their audience. A kind of other-world combination of the Blue Angels and a barnstorming aerial circus.

Three of them stopped in midair and fell toward the ground. Just when it seemed that there must be a tremendous impact, they came to a complete stop and hovered, causing a huge displacement of air that thundered and roared and rumbled across the canyon.

The objects were making no sounds by themselves now, but their gravity-defying manoeuvres were creating thunder that rattled the cubicles, the instruments within, short-circuiting several of the computers, and everyone's brains. The lights! The heat! So hot that some of the paper debris caught fire as the vehicles carried out their low, swooshing passes over the field.

They played games. Two formations headed breakneck straight ahead toward each other. Just as a massive head-on collision seemed inevitable, the objects somehow filtered through each other, sweeping up, barrel-rolling and swooping back down again.

Down on the field, the scientists were scurrying

out of the way of the things, shouting such cries as 'Duck! Duck!' and 'Shit!'

Some of the objects seemed to have been designed by a cosmic art-deco genius; others looked like flying Christmas trees, coloured lights everywhere.

Gradually, a new thing – resembling the bottom of an electric griddle, bright red and blinking – moved out over the base at an agonizingly slow five miles per hour. It was travelling very low and sucking up – apparently magnetically – everything loose that was metal: clipboards, pen, spectacles, and headsets right off the technicians' heads, cigarette lighters out of their pockets, soda pop cans. One fellow grabbed his mouth as a loose filling flew out of his dental work and stuck to the bottom of the red thing.

Suddenly, the vehicle flashed a blue colour, and everything it had sucked up was let go and fell in a pile onto the ground.

Lacombe walked casually over after it had released its booty and stuck his hand up. The Frenchman walked directly under the strange thing, reached up and actually touched its bottom. It was not hot, but it must have been ticklish, for as soon as Lacombe touched it, it jumped up, scattering the technicians with their cameras and heat-sensory devices and other instruments who had followed Lacombe, and flew off towards the heavens so suddenly that it left behind an enormous thunderclap, which smashed several cubicle windows and scared the hell out of everyone.

Neary was more thrilled than scared. 'I've got to get closer,' he told her.

'I know you do,' she said. 'This is close enough for me.'

'I've got to get down there. Won't you come just a little bit further?'

'No, Roy. I'll wait here.'

'I gotta get down there,' he said, almost apologetically.

'I know,' Jill said. 'I really know. I really know what you want to do.'

They looked at each other closely, sadly. And for the first time since they had known each other they kissed.

Then they parted.

Jillian climbed thirty feet back up the cliff to a small wooded area where she felt she might be more protected and would not be seen by the figures below.

Neary started the long, dangerous scramble down.

TWENTY-SIX

As Roy clambered down the edge of the mountain, he noticed that the display was over. As though some signal had been given, all the objects flew off into the night.

Now in the background, coming out of the low clouds, a hundred points of light flared up around the entire twenty-mile perimeter of the box canyon. Although these light points were hovering at least ten miles away, Neary could tell they were large nuts and bolts vehicles, just hanging there, seeming to guard the perimeter of the base. Now they rose up higher in the sky and dimmed their lights. Roy could barely make out the black shapes behind the glow. It was very eerie.

Things got stranger still.

Down in the stadium, everyone was now exhausted. They were out of breath, picking themselves and their equipment up, brushing off their clothes. Scientists or not, they had all been going through a total culture shock, and each man was trying to handle it, deal with it.

There was no conversation. The wind had dropped off completely now, and the silence was total.

Neary had kept coming all this time and was now on the floor of the mountain, edging his way toward the perimeter of the base when something made him stop and look up.

From behind the mountain and from inside a cloud, something began coming out of the cloud that was completely black. It was not only black but it was huge. So huge that Roy could not comprehend its size. As the huge black shape came over the top of the mountain, blotting out the moon and casting a shadow that crawled over everybody in the canyon, Neary thought he was going to pass out.

Inside the base, the master of ceremonies murmured 'Oh, my God!' and fell to his knees.

'Holy shit!' Laughlin exclaimed, not hearing himself.

Lacombe stared transfixed. '*Mon Dieu*!' he said, realizing that if they could measure this shape, this thing, that it would be over a mile wide and the length of it, covering the entire sky, was still unknown because the end of it was not in sight.

Suddenly it turned on. A surgical sliver of light circumscribed the underside of the thing, and then something opened – some round circle of light exploded, like a corona of light.

It was the size of a city, Neary thought. Indianapolis. No, bigger. Detroit. The top of it looked like an oil refinery, with huge tanks and pipes and blazing fires and working lights everywhere. The phantom mass, sliding across the canyon, seemed somehow old and dirty. It looked junky, like an old city or an immense old ship that had been sailing the skies for hundreds, thousands, millions of years. Neither Roy nor any of the scientists or technicians – or anyone else on earth, for that matter – had ever seen or even imagined anything like it.

As it came over the base, a huge explosion of light flared out behind it and separated into what looked like a thousand brilliant fireflies, except that each 'firefly' was a small (by comparison) vehicle acting like a tugboat. Each 'tugboat' flashed different colours and the thousand of them together formed a scaffold of many-coloured lights onto which the phantom mass – two miles long and a mile wide – seemed to settle. The mass made a slight list as the scaffold – crossbeams blinking colours – escorted it to a landing area of its own far downfield.

Neary had vaulted over the six-foot retaining wall and was now wedged in among the technicians and scientists, all of whom were simply stunned by what they were seeing.

The scaffolding guided the mass down, squishing and shattering about a mile of the landing co-ordinate lights. It was so big that as it settled the leading edge of the mass formed a roof over the top of the entire camp.

The mass has created its own negative gravity field, and within a moment everyone and everything became about forty per cent weightless. Somehow it cheered everyone up. They started bouncing and cavorting buoyantly in the air, some of the more athletic doing cartwheels and somersaults, hanging in the air like Dr. J., their colleagues in jumpsuits sliding and bouncing beneath them with their cameras, snapping pictures of the whole incredible thing.

After the mass was down, the team around the synthesizer individually and collectively felt very faint. They were experiencing the essence of culture shock, despite the years of anticipation and preparation for just this moment.

Lacombe and the Team Leader were the first to

recover partially. They decided to move the synthesizer, which was mounted on casters, closer to the mass. After they had rolled it about seventy-five feet downfield, the members of the team, still feeling other-worldly and unglued, plugged themselves in again.

The master of ceremonies spoke as dispassionately as he could into his pencil microphone. 'All departments at operational during this phase signify by beeping twice.'

Two tones rang across the canyon, startling the utter silence.

The booth technician asked, 'Is the audio analyzer ready? On a standby?'

The master of ceremonies, regaining some equilibrium now that he was doing something, said, 'If everything is ready here on the dark side of the moon, play the five tones.'

Shakespeare played the five notes very slowly.

There was no response from the phantom mass.

'*Encore,*' Lacombe ordered.

The five notes sounded through the night.

The great ship made a sound. It sounded like a pig grunting.

'Must have been something she ate,' the Team Leader said nervously.

The musician/engineer started playing the five notes again.

No response at all this time.

'Again,' the Team Leader said.

Shakespeare started playing.

Suddenly the last two notes were completed by the great mother ship. The noise was incredible. It blew the men back on their heels and shattered all the windows in all the cubicles. The booth technicians ducked the flying glass and some were cut, but too involved even to notice.

'Okay,' the Team Leader said, after a moment. 'Play it again.'

The synthesizer sounded and the ship responded. This time lights – matching the scoreboard's – flashed brilliantly across its surface.

Jillian Guiler knew she could not take any more of this alone. Frightened as she was, she felt it better to try to come down and find Neary. She needed to be with someone to help her survive all this. Jill picked up her little satchel and her Instamatic camera and started climbing down, following the path that Roy had taken.

The master of ceremonies said to Shakespeare and the booth technician, 'Give her six quavers, then pause.'

The musician played the notes.

The ship echoed these notes and then played a group of new notes that none of them had ever heard before.

The booth technician said, 'She gave us four quavers. A group of five quavers. A group of four semiquavers.'

Shakespeare imitated the ship's notes.

The ship added five new notes and five different colours.

Inside the computer cubicles, the technicians were in a sort of Nirvana. The ship was teaching them their musical and chromal vocabulary.

As the exchanges increased in complexity and speed, the computers took over from Shakespeare. He took his hands away from the keys and the

Moog was played by the computers, like a player piano.

'Take everything from the lady,' the M.C. instructed the booth technician. 'Follow her pattern note for note.'

The mother ship exploded with sound and colour and the Moog, in interlock with the computer and the colour scoreboard, was playing right back. For several ecstatic minutes the great ship, the Moog and the scoreboard were actually jamming, like some sort of cosmic rock and light show.

It was very strange music – at one moment melodic and the next atonal, sometimes jazzy, then a little country-and-western, and the next moment something so grotesque and unmusical to their ears that they had to turn away.

Neary was smiling. He did not notice that Jill was now working her way through the crowd. Some of the technicians were clapping, some holding their heads. Lacombe had a dazed, glazed expression.

Suddenly, the ship stopped. It gave a few grunts, and then went silent. All its lights went out.

The base was deadly still and dark for a few moments.

And then the ship started opening.

The whole bottom end of it, beginning with a circumscribed sliver of surgical white light, opened into a furnace of light.

Everyone turned away. They put on their dark glasses and turned back. But even through their sunglasses it was hard to look directly into that burning light.

The thing opened more.

That was too much. Everyone moved back fast.

They moved away from the unnerving light, which was now about one hundred and fifty yards wide.

The opening kept expanding.

First Lacombe, then Neary, and then the others stepped forward again. The white light gave off an intense heat, and then stopped.

Inside the bright heat they could see some movement.

The light was so bright that it sent rays out in all directions. Now there seemed to be eight different figures materializing out of the light. They seemed to be completely inhuman because the white light ate away their bodies into thin strips.

Then they were out of the ship and out of the light.

Lacombe walked toward them.

He – and the others – now saw that they were people. Men.

'I am Claude Lacombe,' the Frenchman said to the group.

The men appeared utterly dazed. They were dressed in 1940s naval air suits. They were all very young and several of them were holding leather helmets and flight goggles in their hands.

They continued to walk forward numbly, in complete shock.

The first man stopped, half-saluted, and said, 'Frank Taylor. Lieutenant J.G. United States Navy Reserve. 064199.'

The M.C. stepped forward and shook his hand. 'Lieutenant, welcome home. This way to debriefing.'

Two men led the lieutenant away.

Neary was having a very hard time taking all this

in. He noticed for the first time a large lightboard with perhaps a hundred black-and-white photographs fixed to it.

'Harry Ward Craig. Captain, United States Navy, 043431.'

'Captain, would you come right this way?'

'Welcome back, Navy,' the team leader said 'Welcome back.'

'Craig, Harry Ward,' a man in a civilian suit said. 'Captain, United States Navy, 043431,' another said, consulting a clipboard. 'Disappeared off Chicken Shoals. Flight Number 19.'

The first civilian went over to the lightboard and put a piece of tape over Craig's picture.

'Matthew McMichael. Lieutenant, United States Naval Reserve, 0909411.'

'Lieutenant. Good to have you back.'

Now more and more figures were emerging out of the intense light.

One of the civilians, staggered by it all, said to the Team Leader, 'They haven't even aged! Einstein *was* right.'

'Einstein was probably one of them.'

There were now more than two hundred returnees coming dazedly out of the great mother ship. They were being immediately corralled by technicians, medical personnel, some civilian officials and taken to the windowless cubicles. On top of each cubicle, Neary noticed, was a sling and hook. He guessed that the people, cubicles and all, would be airlifted away by the big army helicopters when all this was over.

As Roy turned back, he saw Jillian Guiler rushing forward. A tiny figure about three feet tall was running out of the light. It was Barry.

Jillian was laughing and crying as she ran. She embraced the boy, saying, 'Yes! Yes!'

Barry was very happy to see his mother. They were hugging and kissing, and Neary, standing away from them, was thrilled.

Jillian carried the little boy off to the side. They sat together on a little table, and Barry said, 'I went up in the air and I saw our house.'

'I saw you going up in the air,' Jill told him. 'Did you see me running after you?'

'Yeah.'

Roy Neary walked over to Lacombe, who had not noticed him until now. The Frenchman was impressed, in fact, he was delighted that Neary had made it after all.

'Monsieur Neary,' he said, 'what do you want?'

'I just want to know it's really happening.'

Lacombe thought that just the right answer, because the Frenchman was convinced that, in his way, Neary was an even more important breakthrough than this entire encounter. He left Neary standing there, looking at the great ship, and went over to where David Laughlin and several of the Mayflower Project officials were gathered.

'We have to speak about Mr. Neary's case,' Lacombe began in French.

As Laughlin translated, they all noticed that the ship's huge opening was starting to close.

Barry saw it too. 'Are they going away?' he asked his mother.

'Yes, they're going away, Barry. Are you going to stay with me?' Jillian asked him.

'Yes.'

'Forever and ever till you grow up.'

The little boy just laughed delightedly.

Lacombe, Laughlin, and the Mayflower officials were having a heated argument, all talking simultaneously.

Laughlin put up his hand for quiet, and said, 'He says these are ordinary people under extraordinary circumstances. They are *not* special cases.'

Lacombe spoke rapidly again in French.

Translating, Laughlin said, 'These people have given up their lives, their families to come all the way to this meeting. They have been implanted with the vision of this mountain, obsessed. Now it is very important that Mr. Neary, as quickly as possible and voluntarily, be made a part of this project.'

The M.C. protested. 'But we've put our own people through ninety-seven months of intensive training. You can't possibly expect somebody to overcome this gap. I mean, how is he going to adapt, how is he going to handle it all?'

The ship's opening had closed completely.

Barry started to cry. 'Goodbye,' he called. 'Goodbye.' He waved and Jillian started to cry, too.

Apparently, Lacombe had made his case successfully, because the Frenchman left the group and approached Roy again. He shook the bewildered American's hand, and said, 'Monsieur Neary, I envy you.'

At that moment, the great ship opened up again with an explosion of light and sound. BING-BONG it went. BING-BONG, as if calling for attention. All the metal in the base rattled at those giant tones.

Something was coalescing again in the fiery interior of the star ship. Swirling bursts of energy were coming together, twining in helix forms until they seemed to . . . jell.

A figure stood there. Then another. Then a third.

They took a step forward. A single note of sound shot out of the carrier ship like the blare of a thousand trumpets. The three figures took another step forward.

They were immense, eight or nine feet tall. Terribly thin. Too thin for the inner mechanics of the human body, except they resembled humans because they moved on things like legs and waved things like arms.

Jillian picked up a protesting Barry and started moving swiftly away toward the rear of the base. She wasn't taking any chances again. She'd thought she could face anything now that she had Barry, but these creatures were too much.

They took another step forward and then stopped and touched each other. When they touched, they started to glow all over: light was shooting out from their figures. They stood there, touching, swaying, glowing, and then one of them seemed to reach out an incredible long armlike thing and pointed it at Roy.

Neary seemed confused and moved several steps away from the armlike thing. But it followed, seeming to home in on him. It was definitely pointing at him.

Now Lacombe was also pointing at Roy, nodding at him encouragingly.

The M.C. said, 'Mr. Neary, I am told we can

count on your complete cooperation. What type of blood do you have?'

'I don't have the slightest idea,' Neary said.

The M.C. led Roy over to one of the cubicles. They entered it.

'What is your date of birth?'

'December 4, 1947.'

'Have you ever been inoculated against small-pox, diphtheria . . . ? Is there any history of liver disease in your family?'

Jill, carrying Barry in her arms and her small satchel over one shoulder, had left the base camp and was climbing back to the mountain when she heard a new sound below her and turned to look back down.

From within the great space vehicle a great twittering sound emerged. The space within seemed to convulse, writhing with energy. Small forms began to emerge and make their way through the fiery opening.

They seemed about three feet high, humanoid in that they had arms and legs and a kind of bulbous head. But each figure was hard to distinguish because it was silhouetted against the fiery yellow-white furnace of the mother craft. Their arms and legs were incredibly flexible in a way no human could imitate.

They were infinitely extensible, too, as Lacombe soon discovered. One of the tiny visitors wrapped an arm around him and the arm kept growing longer until it completely encircled the Frenchman's waist.

At first, there was a certain tentativeness about the visitors. They seemed to be testing their shapes against those of the humans, but they also seemed to be testing the reception the humans would give them.

Touch was the key. They touched everywhere, everything. And since touch is something humans react to differently, some of the jumpsuited technicians recoiled and some responded in friendlier fashion.

Inside one of the larger cubicles, which had been designed to resemble a small chapel, a strange service was taking place. Twelve men, in red jumpsuits, holding helmets, with life-support packs on their backs, were kneeling in front of another man dressed in a white jumpsuit.

'May the Lord be praised at all times,' the priest intoned.

'May God grant us a happy journey,' the astronauts responded.

'Lord, show us your ways.'

'And lead us along your path.'

'Oh, that our lives be bent.'

'And keeping our precepts.'

In another cubicle, Neary was now dressing in a red jumpsuit similar to the astronauts'.

'Mr. Neary,' the M.C. was saying, 'our staff has prepared a few basic documents that need your signature. This first just states that you have requested special status within the Mayflower Project of your own volition and have not been coerced into participating.'

Outside, the touching was not only general now, but specific. The visitors were feeling human groins, human faces, human backsides. If the human didn't like it, they moved on to someone who did. And if the human responded by touching them back, the humanoid visitors seemed to swoon for an instant, blinking through a dozen colours and vibrating from dark to bright.

Once they realized they were among 'friends,' the humanoids turned loose in an orgy of touching, palpating, feeling, stroking. A crew chief in a white jumpsuit ripped open a crate of canned Cokes and began popping the tops, handing them to the tiny beings and showing them how to drink from the cans.

The humanoids responded by pouring the Coke into their hands, where it disappeared. The result was instantaneous: humanoids began popping up and down like ping pong balls turned on in a way that Coke had never turned on a human.

On a ledge above this extraordinary happening, Jillian and Barry watched. Jillian dug into her satchel and took out her little camera. She started snapping away. Barry was giggling again, telling his mother about his little friends below.

Lacombe seemed to be a centre of general humanoid affection, probably because he was responding tactilely, stroking when stroked, touching when touched. He was laughing. David Laughlin, beside him also similarly engaged, was laughing.

Inside the chapel, the priest was still intoning, 'God has given his angels' charge over you. Grant these pilgrims, we pray, a happy journey.' But the twelve astronauts' attention had wandered to the large window. They could see and hear snatches of the extraordinary goings-on outside. Not even their ninety-seven months of intensive training had prepared them for all this. Prayer was all right as far as it went, they were all feeling, but soon they were going to be on their own. To a man, they were all very frightened.

Inside Neary's cubicle, the M.C. was still going on. 'This last document is merely a formality. You see, we have a possible problem in the area of canon and common jurisprudence outside of the parameters of our astronomy. The case could be made that you are, in effect, technically speaking . . . dead. This paper just certifies that should such a judgment be rended, that you will accept it. It's merely a formality.'

Roy didn't know what the hell the guy was talking about or what papers he found himself signing. He just wanted to get back out there where all the action was. He was afraid he might be missing something.

He caught sight of the twelve astronauts filing out of the chapel, and then he and the master of ceremonies left their cubicle and joined the procession. The M.C. kept on briefing him feverishly, giving him a cassette player and a satchel full of tapes. A medical technician was listening to his heart through a stethoscope while they walked, and someone else was checking the electrodes in his suit and testing the portable transmitter that was hooked up through a battery pack to the computers in the medical cubicle.

Now the priest was chanting again. 'By the guidance of a star, grant these pilgrims, we pray, a happy journey and peaceful days so that with Your divine angel as their guide they may reach their destination and finally come to the haven of everlasting salvation. God, who led Your servant Abraham out of Ur of the Chaldeans and kept him safe in all his wanderings, may it please You, we pray, also to watch over these servants of Yours ...'

The procession was now surrounded by dozens of little visitors, chittering and blinking. Obviously, they wanted the line to halt.

The priest stopped walking, but continued chanting in a louder monotone. Clearly, he was also very, very frightened. 'Be to them, Lord, a help in their preparations, comfort on the way, shade in the heat, shelter in the rain and cold, a carriage in tiredness, a shield in adversity, a staff in insecurity, a haven in shipwreck, so that under Your guidance they may happily reach their destination and finally return safe to their homes.'

Two of the humanoids entwined themselves around Roy and separated him from the others. Then they left him standing there alone, as if free to make up his mind. Neary turned, looking for Jill and Barry, but he couldn't find them. Then he spotted Lacombe. They looked at each other a long moment, and the Frenchman nodded his head encouragingly and smiled.

Roy turned and took the first step forward. Then he started walking, at first slowly, then faster toward the ship's negative gravity zone, and the fiery, lighted opening. The twelve astronauts began to follow him.

The little humanoids formed a blinking, twittering file on either side of the column of astronauts and accompanied them up the brilliantly lighted stairway toward the glowing interior of the great mother ship.

One little creature separated himself from the procession and flowed over to Lacombe. He reached out one armlike thing and made the first of the hand signs, corresponding to the first note. Lacombe, deeply moved, responded. Then the creature and the Frenchman went through the other four hand signs.

Lacombe looked down into its ... face. It was changing – from something embryonic, unformed into a face of something a thousand years old. Suddenly, Lacombe knew that all the wisdom, all the super-intelligence, the experience that it had to take to build these vehicles, to travel these millions of light years was there in the aging countenance and the ... yes, the smile ... of this fantastic little creature. Lacombe smiled back, and then the little thing flowed away after the others into the phantom ship.

Neary was almost inside now. Incredibly, he was thinking and hearing a song in his head. It was from *Pinocchio*.

When you wish upon a star,
Makes no difference who you are.
Anything your heart desires will come ... to ...
you.

He took another step up the ramp of fiery brilliance into the centre of the starship. Around him the blaze was almost blinding, yet he seemed to be able to see ... everything. And the music in his head grew louder.

If your heart is in your dream,
No request is too extreme,
When you wish upon a star as dreamers do.

Roy turned to make sure the twelve astronauts

were still with him. Then he waved one last time to Lacombe and to Jillian and Barry. He hoped they could still see him.

Outside, on the cement strip, the figures of Neary, the astronauts, the little creatures were dematerializing into fiery light and energy.

Like a bolt out of the blue
Fate steps in and sees you through.
When you wish upon a star your dream . . . comes
. . . true.

Neary walked forward again, leading the way deep into the fiery heart of the mystery.

The great, brilliant opening started sliding shut.

Lacombe, Laughlin and the others stood silently, watching.

And then, slowly at first, then faster, the great phantom starship began to lift off, easing away from its scaffold of light. The scaffold started to rise up around it. Soon it formed a brilliant, multicoloured stairway up to the heavens, and the huge black ship, glowing at the edges now, rose up through layer after layer of clouds. Until this great city in the sky became the brightest of the brightest stars.

Jillian and Barry watched it all together. Jillian took one last picture of it all, the last of the most important pictures in the history of the world. The indisputable proof.